RISE OF THE TEMPLE GODS
HEIR to KOLOSO

Works by K.L. Bone

Rise of the Temple Gods Series
Rise of the Temple Gods: Heir to Kale
Rise of the Temple Gods: Heir to Koloso
Rise of the Temple Gods: Heir to the Defendants (coming 2016)

The Black Rose Series
Black Rose
Heart of the Rose
Blood Rose
Silver Rose (coming soon)

Other Novels
The Indoctrination

RISE OF THE TEMPLE GODS
HEIR to KOLOSO

K.L. BONE

Heir to Koloso Copyright © 2015 by Kristin L. Bone
ALL RIGHTS RESERVED.

Cover Art © 2015 by Skyla Dawn Cameron

Illustrated Map © 2016 by Raven Quinn

First Edition: March 2015

All rights reserved under the International and Pan-American Copyright Conventions. No part of this book may be reproduced or transmitted in any form or by any means, electronic or mechanical including photocopying, recording, or by any information storage and retrieval system, without permission in writing from the author.

This book is a work of fiction. Names, characters, places and incidents are either the product of the author's imagination or are used fictitiously, and any resemblance to any actual persons, living or dead, events, or locales is entirely coincidental.

Dedication

This novel is dedicated to my loving husband, Cameron, who has stood by my side through the writing process and for his never-ending love and support.

To my friends who never fail to encourage and inspire: Greg, Becket, and Stacey.

And to my brother, Sam, who played in the land of Kale long before it was ever committed to paper—Thanks for all the memories.

Prologue

Almost 26 Years Ago

The temple of Ziazan hosted a tournament once every thirteen years. It was an exclusive event, where only proven Royal Champions of the previous twelve tournaments were invited to compete. To the winner went fortune, title, eternal glory, and above all, admittance to the Kalian Defendant Team. In the history of this sacred event, only one man had ever won all thirteen of these tournaments. After today, there would be another.

The crowd gathered to witness the impending fight was larger than any had ever seen. People swarmed, crushing themselves against the bodies of others in hopes of gaining even the slightest glimpse of what was sure to be the fight of the century. In the top level boxes reserved for those of royal and temple status, there was not an empty seat. Every defendant, temple master, high-ranking student, lord and lady had gathered for this event. Seated across from the tournament mats in an isolated box set slightly higher than most of the crowd, sat King Nicholas Dektra, dressed in satin robes of deep crimson along with his eldest son, Crown Prince Darek. To their left in matching robes of gold sat High Priest Seth, Lord of the Kalian Temples and spiritual leader to the Gods along with Master Michael, Master of Kale and a former Golden Defendant.

A sense of anticipation filled the air and all seemed to be holding their breath waiting for the final match to begin. Lady Annabelle had just been defeated by both of the champions who were preparing to face off, taking her place as the third best fighter and highest ranking woman in the land. Now all that remained was to see which of the remaining two fighters would win the title Champion of the Kalian Temples.

Normal tournaments were fought in pairs, two on two. However, at the thirteenth tournament, teams disappeared and partnerships dissolved, each man fighting one on one to prove himself worthy of being call the greatest fighter in the land. Lord Leonardo and Prince Eadmund of Kale had been partners for over fifteen years. Today, for the first time, they would face each other on the temple mats and at long last, discover who was the best.

Down a dark marble hallway, standing in front of a silver mirror, stood Lord Leonardo Desato. His blond hair was cut short and his jade green eyes seemed darker than normal in the dim light of the borrowed bedroom. He was dressed in long satin pants and a long sleeve shirt also of satin. The sleeves were cinched tightly at his wrists but remained loose and comfortable along his arms. The material was designed in elaborate circles of gold, silver, red, pink, black, yellow, green, blue, white, purple and then back to gold, swirling around him with all the colors of the Kalian Temples. All Royal Champions invited to compete in this monumental event had worn the same.

Prince Eadmund stood before a similar mirror, buttoning the last of his sleeves to his pale wrists. His height a few inches over six feet, the prince stood at an exact match to his long-time partner. Eadmund's deep-set blue eyes appeared sapphire in firelight. His brown hair, usually kept long, had been cut close for this occasion, and his usual silver robes were discarded for the rainbow status of his Royal Championship rank.

Eadmund was grateful for the respite that had been granted after his last fight with Lady Annabelle. The former golden student of Koloso had proven herself more than worthy of the fierce reputation which had preceded her. Three years older than the prince, Lady Annabelle had left the tournament a year before Leo and Eadmund had entered, taking her place on the Defendant Team where she now served. It was both champions' hope that after this fight, they would also be offered placement upon this most coveted of teams.

"Well," the prince said, turning to his longtime partner. "I guess it's all or nothing now."

"Look on the bright side." Leo turned with a smile. "No matter who wins, neither of us has to marry Annabelle."

Eadmund laughed softly. "Ah, yes, that would be my brother's privilege now."

"Poor bastard. Still, as far as Kolosians go... Did you see those eyes?"

"Pale, pale blue, like ice on the highest mountains. No wonder they call her the ice princess."

"Well, it will be ice *queen* once she marries your brother."

"Very true." Eadmund gave a slight laugh.

"Still, could you imagine yourself tangled up in that long black hair?"

Eadmund swung lightly at Leo's left arm, but Leo stepped back, his arm swept through the air. "Are you allowed to fantasize about the future queen?"

"Only until she actually is queen," Leo replied. "If she were Kalian, I might have fought your brother for her."

Eadmund sighed. "I know. I was really hoping that Joanna would beat her for the top slot. It makes me a little nervous, considering my brother's lack of training or temple loyalty. Next thing you know, the royal children will grow up Kolosian."

Leo visibly shuddered. "The high priest would never allow it."

"Thank the Gods. Still, I wonder how my brother is going to handle her. She might be too much for him."

"Well, at least we don't have to worry about it, do we?"

"No, I suppose not."

Leo glanced up at the clock on the side of the wall. "Looks like it's almost time."

"Yes. I suppose we should be heading that way." The two men's gazes met.

"No matter what happens," Leo began.

"I know." Eadmund offered a smile. "We are Kalian."

"Partners...to the end."

Chapter I

THERE ARE NO GRAVES FOR fallen defendants, merely a pile of ash that is scattered by the powerful winds eternally sweeping across the Rainbow Mountains and acknowledgement on a large, marble wall upon which the names of fallen heroes are forever etched. The name of every defendant who had ever died in service to the realm could be found upon this wall, their names separated by neither temple nor rank, but instead coexisting in a simplistic unity upon the ancient tiles. Today, Princess Ameria watched as the names of Prince Eadmund Dektra and Lord Leonardo Desato were added to the perpetual list of the fallen.

"Partners to the end," Ameria whispered as she stared at the expanse of white tiles. "Who would have thought, after all the years of estrangement, that their names would lie forever side-by-side."

"Their ashes consumed within a single flame." Master Jiro was standing beside the princess. His long silver robes were wrapped tightly against the biting gusts, an almost perfect complement to the gray streaks within his short brown hair. "It seems appropriate, as it should be."

"Appropriate?" Ameria sounded surprised. "Those two despised each other."

The Kolosian master shook his head and turned his eyes upon the princess. "I wish you could have seen them, Ameria."

"Of course," she replied. "Their fight is, after all, legendary."

Jiro shook his head. "Not to me. Let others remember that match, princess." A bittersweet smile came to his lips. "Watching those two fight against each other was nothing compared to the privilege of watching them battle together. The thrill of knowing that, as long as they stood together, no force could stop them." His eyes trailed back to the tall memorial, luminous despite the fading late afternoon light. "Prince Eadmund and Lord Leonardo were a sight to behold."

"They had not been partners for years! They were not even friends."

"No, they were more. They were brothers, Kalian brothers." He shifted his gaze back to Ameria's. "What I pray you will one day come to learn, my lady, is that friendships may be born in common interests, or perhaps by destiny in general, but they grow through shared hardship. Only through anger can one truly know love. Only through darkness can one appreciate the light. Your father and his partner learned that the hard way." He drew a deep breath. "I wish you could have seen them. They were partners...to the bitter end."

CHAPTER II

TEARS FELL FROM THE SKY.

Mary knelt in the dank, blue grass. The night surrounded her with unrelenting darkness. The wraith's hot, putrid breath warmed her cheek against the bitter cold.

"Why?" she asked into the wraith's deep, reflective eyes.

"Mary," a voice whispered through the darkness.

"Marcus?" Her eyes sought the familiar voice.

"They killed me, Mary. You let them kill me."

"No, I..."

"You chose him."

"I didn't. I didn't want..."

His shape began to take substance, the darkness lightening around his tall frame. "You let me die, Mary."

"No. I didn't want this!"

"It was your choice!" His words filled the air as he fell to the ground, blood spilling from unseen wounds. She rushed to his side. Blood seemed to be everywhere, seeping from the very pores of his pale skin.

"Marcus!" she cried, gathering his heavy form in her arms, heedlessly smearing her garments in his thick, wet blood. A sharp coppery tang overrode the musk of decay. "Marcus!"

"Death, princess." The wraith's voice slid over her. "Death to those who love you."

Mary screamed in response to the sharp knock on her bedroom door. A guard entered the room, offering a low bow. "Forgive me, Your Highness. I did not mean to startle you, but Lord Kyle of Koloso is here."

Several deep breaths were required to calm the frantic beating of her heart. "Give me two minutes," she instructed, "then send him in." In acknowledgement, the guard again bowed before leaving the room.

With efficient movements, she rose from the bed and pulled a thick golden robe around her before straightening lofty golden covers over matching sheets. Moments later, Kyle entered the room and knelt before his acting sovereign. "My princess."

"Kyle." Her voice was soft. "There is something I must do in the coming days, for which I require an honor guard."

"Yes, princess. I am aware."

"As the son of a high lord of the realm and as a representative of the Temple of Koloso, I would like for you to join me as the temporary captain of my guard."

Kyle raised his head, turning his jade green eyes upon the princess. Her breath caught at the sight of the long, jagged scar that ran both above and below his emerald eye, marring once perfect skin.

"My lady?" His voice was like a velvet caress.

She took a step, but was stopped by a sinister whisper. "*Death.*"

"Mariana?"

"Kyle." His name rose on the edge of a breath. A chill crawled over her skin. "I need you, Kyle."

He remained in his kneeling position. "What would you have of me, my lady?"

"I need you to act like a knight of the realm and harden your gaze." She fought to control her voice. "I am trying to be a queen. And I cannot do that with you looking at me as you are now; gazing up with those sad, pained eyes. I would ask another, but you are the best. In this moment, I need you to serve the realm so that I can do the same."

"My princess." He rose from the floor in an elegant sweep of his silver robes. "I will always serve the realm." The words, "*And you,*" filled the space between them, though they were not spoken.

Kyle turned from his sovereign and walked silently toward the door. She watched him go, nails indenting half-moons into her palms as she fought the urge to call out his name.

Chapter III

Princess Ameria walked toward the tall golden door of the Temple of Kale. As she entered the swirling rainbow halls, she was greeted by a tall woman with shoulder-length brown hair and golden eyes. She was dressed in traditional Kalian robes with the temple's crest—a thin golden sword encircled with Kale's golden crown—upon her breast. "Master Julie," Ameria addressed the assistant Master of Kale.

"My Lady of Koloso." Julie gave a slight bow before her. "To what do I owe this honor?"

Ameria observed the Kalian master for several moments and then stepped forward. "Let's go into one of the common rooms," the princess said. "It has been a long ride and I would like to sit down for a few moments, if you don't mind."

"Of course, my lady." Julie turned and followed her down the long series of hallways until they emerged into one of the sitting rooms. The walls of the room were lined with large paned windows. Light from all three of Kale's suns filled the room, glistening off the gold satin furniture which stood against the back wall. Ameria moved to the two couches on the left side of the room and seated herself on the satin edge, her own golden robes blending in with the cloth beneath her. Master Julie took a seat across from her.

"Tell me," the princess addressed the Kalian master. "Are you to be named the new leader of the Kalian temple?"

"I'm uncertain," Julie replied.

"No," Ameria stated. "Of course not."

"Why would you…" Julie cleared her throat. "Temple leaders are chosen by Lord Louis and he has yet to make a decision. Unless you know something that I do not, my lady."

"Tell me this," Ameria replied. "Do you think you will be named the new temple leader?"

"I would be honored to assume such a position," Julie replied.

Ameria considered speaking more, but decided to allow the older woman to hold on to her dreams of grandeur a bit longer. To her it was all too clear. The thirteenth tournament was coming soon, and in all likelihood, the twin Princesses of Kale would face off in the final round. The champion would become queen. The runner-up would be invited to join the Kalian Defendants and challenge for the right to the golden leadership. Lady Rebecca respectfully would step down from the team to become the new Temple Master of Kale. The silver member, Stephen, would not stand a chance. The pure simplicity of the plan was brilliant. Lady Rebecca leading the temples, Mariana leading the defendants, and Ameria herself on the throne. It was so perfect. Except...

"Master Julie." Ameria shook her head, drawing herself out of her thoughts. "I'm here to speak with Ryan. It is my understanding he is here."

Tension seemed to stiffen Julie's frame, her back straightened and her shoulders drew closer together. "He is, my princess."

"I am not here to harm him," Ameria said. "Nor am I here to ask questions to which he will not answer. However, I would like to speak with him, if he will consent."

Master Julie stood from the couch, her robes blending in with the scenery behind her and offered a nod. "I shall go ask him."

"Thank you."

Chapter IV

———⋆※⋆———

Princess Mariana sat on the left side of an imposing rectangular table. Across the expanse of finely hewn granite, presided a sea of nameless faces, advisors of the late king. The council had been in session for the better part of two hours, and the voices had long ago blended into a single stream of rhetoric and posturing to which she paid little attention, her mind instead focused upon her recent fight with her sister.

"You are not worthy of the crown," Ameria's words haunted her. *"I claim no sister who allowed my father's murderer to go free."*

Was her sister right? Had she allowed her fear of losing another friend to cloud her judgment? Was her heart too soft to sit upon the throne? The fight had escalated so quickly to violence. She blinked and could again see the edge of her sister's blade sailing towards her, feel the mixture of anger and fear which raced through her as she raised her sword to meet Ameria's challenge, the sound of their clashing steel echoing...

"My princess." Lord Chiro's voice pulled her back to the present.

She shook herself and turned to face the tall man with pale skin and his son's emerald green eyes. "My lady," he stated, "did you hear me?"

"Apologies, my lord. Would you repeat that?"

"I asked if there were any orders that you, as acting queen, had for us."

"No... Yes," Mary shook her head, "actually, can we clear the room, please?"

Clerics and petitioners stood from the table in a flutter of crimson robes and offered low bows in her direction. As they began to file out of the room, Mary called, "Chiro, would you please wait a moment? I would like to speak with you privately."

"Yes, Your Highness," Chiro replied before returning to the large table as he waited for the crowd to disperse into the hallways. When he finally moved back toward the metallic-flecked stone table, he was alone with the princess.

"My lord," she addressed the older man. "You have long served this realm both as a former defendant and as a high lord. I would now ask of you another service."

"What would you have of me?"

Mary drew a deep breath. "As you know, I was raised in the temples. As such, I know little of court politics. However, I do know what direction my uncle has taken this kingdom, and I do not approve of our current trajectory. It is time for a change. And in this monumental task, I require your assistance."

"Of course, my lady."

Pushing the carved dark wooden chair behind her, she stood and walked toward the opposite side of the room, stretching her legs. "The first issue involves my uncle's political advisors. They have more than served their purpose under my uncle's reign, and should be dismissed."

Lord Chiro nodded before asking, "Which advisors would you like to dismiss?"

"All of them."

"All?"

She turned her gaze upon the older man. "Yes. I would dismiss them all, and ask that you take their place as the leader of my Royal Council."

Lord Chiro dropped down to one knee and entered the traditional temple bow. "It would be my honor, Princess of Kale."

Princess of Koloso," the wraith's voice whispered through the room, though whether she actually heard the words, or if they instead rose from the recesses of her mind, she was uncertain.

"In addition to yourself, I will also be appointing Lord Jiro of Koloso, Lady Rebecca of Kale, Lady Laciety of Kale, and Lord Lester of Critous. This group shall serve as my royal advisors and advise me in all matters of crown and state."

"Have you spoken with the other candidates?"

"All but Lady Laciety."

"The Lady of Sectra? The mother of your fallen teammate?"

She paused to draw breath. "Yes."

"I have met the Lady of Sectra on a number of occasions. She would make a fine addition to your council."

A brief smile answered his assessment. "In the meantime, I would like for you to greet the coming advisors and ensure that rooms are properly provided. Once my new council is in place, dismiss my uncle's advisors immediately."

"My princess, if I may ask, is it wise to pursue these actions with the question of the crown hanging upon the thirteenth tournament?"

"That tournament is still many months away. I will not declare myself queen until I have defeated my sister, as is traditional, but I also will not allow these lands to continue its decline." Mary brushed her long black hair from her face, tucking a few stray strands behind her left ear. "If this is going to be my only chance to rule, I intend to not let it go to waste. Things are going to change, my lord. Starting with this group of so-called advisors."

Chiro gave a curt nod. "I will see it done."

"Thank you," she said as Chiro turned to go. "Oh, one more thing. Those temple statues the late king moved to the far side of the palace grounds? I want them moved back to their rightful place, in front of the palace. These grounds will be a stranger to the Gods no longer."

Chapter V

Master Julie led Princess Ameria down a series of hallways to a large purple door and knocked softly. "Come in," Ryan's voice replied from within the small purple room. Julie opened the door and Princess Ameria followed her into the room beyond. Ryan was seated in a straight back chair covered with purple cushions before a large wooden desk, also painted a dark purple. His short black hair was combed back neatly. As they entered, he gazed up at Ameria with his jade green eyes before standing from his chair, towering several inches taller than the princess. Ryan entered into a low Kalian bow, bending to one knee facing the ground while placing both of his arms on either side of his body, touching only his fingertips to the floor.

"Rise," Ameria commanded. Ryan stood in a single movement much more fluid than the last time Ameria had seen him. "Take a seat, Ryan." Ryan moved himself back to the purple desk, turning the chair to face the two visitors. He seated himself into the chair, his dark violet robes blending with the purple cushions.

Ameria quietly pulled up a second chair which was sitting on the left side of the room and moved it several feet in front of Ryan. She then turned to Master Julie. "Leave us," she commanded.

Julie hesitated and Ameria turned to Ryan. "You have my word, on my honor as the Golden Student of Koloso and my status as a Princess of Kale," she fought to control her voice. "I am here only to speak with you. With your permission, I would like to do so alone."

Ryan hesitated for a moment, then nodded to Julie.

"I will be outside if needed," she stated. Then the Kalian Master left the room, closing the large purple door behind her with a soft click. Ameria turned her sapphire eyes on to the emerald ones of the young man seated before her.

"I am not here to ask questions to which you will not give the answer," she told him.

"Then why are you here, my lady?" he asked with an edge of tension in his voice.

Several moments of silence passed, then Ameria said, "What I did to you, Ryan, was what I considered necessary for the protection of my kingdom. Your brother killed my father, and I still remain convinced that you assisted him in doing so. If you are expecting an apology, then you will be disappointed with this meeting."

"You came here and asked to speak with me, my lady. Not the other way around."

She nodded.

"What do you want?"

"I don't understand," she responded in a tight, controlled voice, her fingers digging into the folds of her golden robes. "I want to understand, but I do not."

"My brother killed your father and your sister's master. What else is there to understand?"

Ameria closed her eyes and saw her father's body lying on the funeral pyre before the Kalian Temple of Ziazan. She opened her blue eyes and drew a slow breath, struggling to control her voice as she continued. "Ryan," she tried again. "I understand what happened that day. What I do not understand, is why."

Ryan regarded her suspiciously. "Since when does it matter, why?"

"It matters to me. I am a princess of the realm, and may someday be queen. I want to understand why your brother killed my," she drew another breath, "father. From a practical standpoint, your brother's choice of victims makes no sense."

Ryan straightened in his chair. He titled his head to the left. "My brother killed the heir to the throne and the most powerful of your temple protectors. What doesn't make sense?"

"I know who he killed," she spoke through gritted teeth, then straightened in her chair. "My father and Leo have successors, Ryan. Mary and I are the heirs to the Blood and Arms elements of succession and are both ready and prepared to take our respective places in Kalian society. The Golden Defendant, Lady Rebecca, is prepared to take over the leadership of the temples. What you did, killing my father and Master Leo, practically, makes no sense. You have disrupted neither temple nor throne or the Defendant Team. Twice your brother has met both my sister and myself with a sword in hand and twice, he did not engage us to the best of his obviously skilled ability."

She fought the urge to stand from the chair. "I am your princess, Ryan. If I become queen, your life will lie in my hands. I am asking you,

Ryan, as your princess, why did your brother kill my father and Leo, instead of myself, my sister, or Lady Rebecca?"

Ryan stood from the chair and walked toward the back of the room. She remained still allowing the clearly agitated man time to consider her words. He walked toward the edge of the far wall, then stopped and stared down towards the purple carpet beneath him. Several minutes passed before Ameria finally rose from her chair, gathering herself to her full height. Her golden robes slid around her thin frame with a slight swish of satin. "Thank you for your time."

She turned towards the door when Ryan said, "You don't know, who is he, do you?"

"Your brother?"

"No, my father."

"Your father? Did your father put the three of you up to this?"

Ryan turned back from the room and took several steps towards her, partially closing the distance between them. "My lady," he addressed her. "My father was a defendant. Third in command to Master Leo."

"To Leo?" Ameria said in disbelief.

"His name was Nathaniel Crestal, though most called him Nathan. He was the silver student of Koloso, the class after your mother's. And he was the Red Defendant of Kale."

Ameria bit her lip hard enough to draw blood, fighting the urge to call him a liar. Instead, she walked stiffly back to the violet covered chair and re-seated herself upon the soft cushions. "Tell me more."

Chapter VI

24 Years Ago

Prince Eadmund paced before the large fire. Dressed in crisp silver robes, Eadmund impatiently awaited the arrival of his brother. The Silver Defendant stood in a room on the west side of the palace grounds. The room was large. The walls were painted a deep crimson. Two large sofas sat facing each other across a low table near its center.

Beside the prince stood fellow defendant, Lord Nathaniel, dressed in robes of bright red. The silver mark of Koloso stood on the left side of his robe, in contrast to Eadmund's gold mark of Kale. Nathaniel's skin was as pale as any pure-blooded Kalian. He had the same jade green eyes of his father, the High Lord of Flos and short, jet black hair. He was the eldest son of the Kalian lord, and destined to one day take his father's place. The two men had ridden from the Temple of Kevera directly to the palace, and were now awaiting the arrival of the king, who had ascended the throne three months prior, when King Nicholas V had passed into the realm of the Kalian Gods.

"What is taking so long?" Eadmund grumbled as he continued to pace before the large, crackling fire.

"You might want to try sitting down," Nathaniel advised the Crown Prince. "I don't think pacing is going to make him come any faster."

"I can't believe he was this stupid." Eadmund cursed under his breath before pausing to face Nathaniel. "They might be rumors. There is no actual…"

"The news came from the Lord of Turbamentum." Nathaniel shook his head. "His information network is second to none."

"His spies, you mean." The prince walked across the room toward the large sofas. He took a seat on the edge of the crimson cushions, carefully maneuvering his Kalian blade from his side.

Eadmund turned his head at the sound of the opening door. His brother, King Darek Dektra walked into the room. He stood dressed in a long-sleeved shirt of deep red with small, silver buttons. It was tucked into a pair of black slacks and a black belt blended into the dark attire. He had jade green eyes and sandy brown hair, on which sat a small circlet of gold, marking him as the King of the Kalian Bloodline.

Both defendants stood from the couch and entered into a low bow. "Your Majesty," Eadmund addressed him.

"Rise, my lords," the king responded before moving to offer his brother a light embrace. "It is good to see you, brother. I have not seen much of you since our father's death."

Eadmund nodded, "It has been a busy time for us. Leo has kept me scouting the roads on the outskirts of Periculum."

"Yes." The king nodded. "I have heard that there was some trouble in the area. I sent a group of the palace guards to help assist some of the local villages."

Eadmund nodded. "Yes, and it was much appreciated, Your Majesty."

"Please," the king said with a smile. "You are still my brother."

Eadmund gave a nod and then motioned toward his fellow defendant. "I wonder if you, per chance, remember Lord Nathaniel, the Red Defendant, heir to the province of Flos and former silver member of the Temple of Koloso?"

"Why of course." The king extended a hand to the young lord. "Your father sits upon my Royal Council. My father considered him the most loyal of companions."

"Yes, Your Majesty. My father spoke fondly of King Nicholas. I was sad to hear of his passing."

"Thank you, Nathaniel." The king moved farther into the room and took a seat upon the dark red cushions. The two defendants moved across from him and took a seat as well. "Tell me, brother; to what do I owe the honor of your company?"

Eadmund cleared his throat. "Well, brother," he used the familial title, "I came here today, hoping to dispel a rumor mentioned by one of my fellow defendants."

"Rumor?"

Eadumnd nodded. "You see, brother, it has been brought to my attention, that you violated temple law by marrying a bride from a neighboring province, and in effect breaking your engagement to Lady Annabelle of Serenitas."

"And where, pray, did you hear such a rumor?"

"From, unfortunately, a very reliable source," Eadmund answered. He leaned towards the edge of his cushion. "Brother…tell me this isn't true."

The king straightened, his shoulders slid closer together and his lips closed into a thin line. "We were married a week ago."

The color drained from Eadmund's face and Nathaniel asked, "To whom, Your Majesty?"

"Lady Katerin of Agnus. She is now your Kalian Queen."

"I am unfamiliar with that name," Nathaniel inquired. "Did she train at a lesser temple?"

"No." The king shook his head. "She is not from the temples."

"You married a temple-less bride?" Eadmund looked as though he were going to collapse then and there. He buried his face in his hands. "What have you done? How did you convince a temple leader to marry you without the high priest's consent? Without Master Michael's presence? Without the entire court?" He raised his head. "You're the king for Gods' sakes! How did you have a secret wedding? Do you really think the kingdom will stand for what you have done?"

"The kingdom has no say! I fell in love with a beautiful woman from one of the noblest families in the kingdom. She's as Kalian as we are! Why in the world would I marry Annabelle, a woman who I met for the first time when she was introduced as my intended?"

Eadmund stood from his chair, his hand clutched tightly around the hilt of his sword. "Because it is our most ancient tradition! The land must always be ruled by Blood and Arms. Even our father knew that! And what, exactly, do you plan to tell the Lord of Serenitas when he learns of your slander against him?"

"I expect him to respect my decision, brother. As I expect you to do as well!" The king stood to match his brother's height. "She is your queen now. And you will show her all the courtesy that is due to her. The announcement will be public within the fortnight."

"You are talking about civil war."

"Don't be ridiculous!" Darek shot back. "I think the guards are more than capable of handling Serenitas if the occasion calls for it."

"And Flos," Nathaniel added. The king turned from his brother and looked at the Red Defendant quizzically. "I am engaged to the younger Lady of Serenitas, and as such, my father has a duty to hers."

"Your father has a duty to his king!"

"My parents were the gold and silver students of Koloso." Nathaniel spoke his next words in a voice as neutral as he could manage. "They will follow High Priest Seth and I am afraid that you have offered him a grave insult by allowing yourself to be married outside of Temple law. Also, the

Lord of Turbamentum is married to a lady of Serenitas. You will find little sympathy from him."

"Brother," Eadmund said. "It is not too late. Without the presence of the high priest, you can say that this marriage wasn't real. Renounce it now and we will work to keep the recent events out of the light. If you marry Lady Annabelle quickly, it will seem as though it was a rumor."

The king looked at his brother incredulously. "Are you crazy?" he asked. "I will do no such thing. Katerin is your queen now; my chosen bride. I will not let anyone else dictate such a thing."

"But Darek." Eadmund shook his head. "You can't defy the Gods themselves. No good can come of it."

"I don't give a damn what your temple Gods want. I am not of the temples and shall take no bride who is. It is time for a more civilized ruler to take the throne and I intend to run my kingdom as such!" He walked angrily toward the tall wooden doors.

After he left the room, the two defendants looked at each other in silence before Nathaniel turned toward the prince. "Well, now the question is which one of us is more likely to be able to tell Annabelle?"

"Without losing our necks," Eadmund finished for him.

Chapter VII

Princess Mariana rose early the next morning and dressed into her golden Kalian robes. She brushed out her long black hair and then proceeded to add a thin, gold circle to her brow, marking her royal status. She then called to the guard and asked for her stallion, Sherwyn, to be saddled and brought around to the front of the palace.

"Forgive me, my lady," the guard asked. "Should I assemble an escort for you as well?"

"It won't be necessary," she replied. "I will stay within the walls of the palace grounds."

"Forgive me again, my lady, but after what happened to your father and Master Leo."

She turned her emerald eyes upon him. "I need to clear my head and I can't do that surrounded by the palace guard. Call for my horse."

He hesitated for only a moment before turning to carry out the princess' orders.

"He's right," another voice said from around the corner. "You cannot ride out by yourself." Mary turned to find herself facing a tall man with short brown hair and golden eyes. He wore robes of a deep pink and the silver mark of Koloso stood as though metallic against the satin material. "Please, my lady. Allow me to accompany you on your ride. I will ride silently, if that is your wish."

She paused and then sighed. "Very well, Brandan." A second guard moved toward the door, in all probability to order a second horse to be saddled. "What are you doing here?"

"I accompanied Kyle when he rode out yesterday."

Mary nodded before turning and walking down the long golden corridor toward the outer doors of the palace. Brandan followed a few paces behind her. When they emerged through the doors, she found herself squinting against the bright sunshine as she walked towards her golden stallion. The guard held Sherwyn steady as she stepped to the side and mounted her horse in a single, fluid motion. Beside her, Brandan did the same. She grabbed the reins and turned her horse away from the palace before glancing back to Brandan, who sat astride his own silver mount. "Try to keep up," she told the pink Kolosian as she moved Sherwyn into a soft trot, before transitioning into a run.

The wind bit into her skin and blew through her long black hair. *Mary*, the wind seemed to whisper. *It was your choice.* She slacked her grip on the reins and leaned her body closer to Sherwyn's mane. *Your choice...*

"Faster," she told the golden stallion. The horse increased his pace until she had to close her eyes against the rush of the wind. She leaned even lower into the saddle, the tips of Sherwyn's mane lashing her cheek like a whip, and still, she urged the horse faster. They approached the outer palace gates. Brandan shouted, "Princess!" from somewhere behind her, but she did not look up. The gates opened before their queen and she raced through them, as though trying to outrun the wind itself. She went up and down the grassy hills, not knowing or caring if Brandan kept pace as she tried desperately to outrun the voices nipping at her heels.

When Sherwyn's pace finally slowed, she pulled herself up from his golden neck. Her eyes stung. Tears splattered her face and her hands ached from clinging to the reins. She drew several deep breaths and then turned her head to the left. The wraith stood on the far side of the field. She jerked the reins violently, causing Sherwyn to rise up on his back legs. She fought to keep from being thrown off the horse, wrapping her arms around its neck, as he brought his front hooves back down toward the ground. She turned back toward the left. The wraith was nowhere to be seen.

"Are you there?" she asked no one. She listened for several moments, then heard the sound of hoof beats. She turned her horse, trying to form an apology for Brandan. However, as she gazed across the field of blue grass, it was Kyle who came racing toward her.

"What are you doing here?"

"Shouldn't I be asking you that question, princess? What were you thinking, riding out like that?"

"Where's Brandan?"

"Back at the palace, I assume. There was no way he could keep up with you; but then again, you knew that." He shook his head. "I was touring the palace grounds when I saw you racing for the gate."

She glared at him. "I wanted to clear my head."

"You are the de facto queen, my lady. You can't ride out like that."

"If I am queen, than I can do whatever I like."

"Mary," anger filtered through the Kolosian's voice, "after what happened..."

"I know what happened!" Mary screamed back. "He died in my arms, by the Gods! I know what happened!"

"You are being reckless. Are you trying to get yourself killed as well?"

Anger seared through her like a fire. "Reckless? I am your queen! I am..."

Her rage was interrupted by a short scream. Both heads turned to the left almost instantaneously.

"Did you?" Kyle asked. She nodded. Another scream rose, more audible than the first. Mary turned Sherwyn's reins and began to ride toward the left.

"Mary!" he called. "You can't..."

She ignored him and continued to ride toward the source of the sound. Kyle urged his horse forward and gave chase. When they reached the top of the next hill, she found a large group of men on black horses. Four of the men wore dark robes of purple, which Mary knew marked them as guards to the Province of Usqub. It was a shade darker than the colors worn by the defendants and temple students. They had their swords drawn and pointed in the direction of the two young men who stood between them. She would have guessed they were in their early twenties. They had matching brown hair. One wore a faded red shirt, and the other wore equally faded blue atop matching black pants that did not seem quite long enough for them.

She pulled up on the reins at the top of the hill and turned back to Kyle. "What are members of the Usqub guard doing this far south?"

"Usqub?" he asked. "Are you sure they are from..." Kyle glanced toward the men, instantly recognizing the deep purple robes. "I have no idea."

Mary urged her horse forward as Kyle moved to her side. They rode toward the men, who had pulled their own mounts to a stop at the sight of the gold and silver stallions. They stopped a few feet in front of the men. One of the purple garbed men placed his sword in its sheath and dismounted his horse to offer a bow to the princess.

"These lands are protected by the Palace Guard," she informed the kneeling man. "What business do you have taking prisoners upon it?"

"Forgive me, princess," the guard addressed her, then raised his torso to stare up at his sovereign. "These men," he motioned to the two twenty-year-olds behind him, "are runaways. We have tracked them all the way from the Temple of Bellum."

"On orders to the temple master?"

"No. The order came from the Lord of Usqub."

She returned her gaze to the two prisoners. They appeared even more ragged at a closer glance, their clothes fraying at the edges with the one in the blue shirt sporting a dark bruise on the left side of his face. "What is their crime?" she asked the still kneeling guard.

"They are thieves, my lady."

"He's lying!" the prisoner in the blue shirt called out.

"Be quite, brother," said the other. "She won't help us."

A sudden sound made Mary turn her head. Behind her, Brandan rode up along with his occasional partner, Kev, who was garbed in black satin robes. The two men drew up on their reins behind the princess.

Kyle maneuvered his horse several steps and then asked, "What did they steal? It must have been important for you to chase them all the way from the northern province."

"They stole some gold, my lord. We take theft very seriously in the north."

She exchanged a glance with Kyle before moving her golden stallion past the men surrounding her. She turned and addressed the prisoners directly. "What's your name?"

The man in the blue shirt answered, "Rob, and that's my brother, Cal."

"Did you steal from the northern province?"

"They are the ones who are the thieves," Rob replied.

"She is not going to help us," Cal cautioned him again.

"What do you mean by that?" she asked, ignoring the second brother. When Rob paused, Mary said, "I am the golden student of Kale and the Crown Princess of this kingdom. He," she motioned back to Kyle, "is the silver of Koloso. You have my word, if something is amiss, I will set it right."

The young man knelt to one knee. "Please, my lady. These men ransacked our village, they took our food, medicine, and gold. They said it was in payment to the raised taxes."

She felt her eyes narrow. "Has this happened before?"

"My lady," the guard interrupted. "These thieves would say anything to…"

"Silence," Kyle cut him off. "The princess has not given you permission to speak."

Mary dismounted her horse and walked closer to Rob. She knelt beside the young man and turned his gaze to meet her own. "Rob," she asked softly, "did you come to the southern province for help?"

He nodded. "They guard the borders and kill anyone who tries to leave. They've done it for years."

She glanced back to where Kyle stood, suddenly grateful for the arrival of the Kolosian teammates. She walked toward Sherwyn, strategically placing her hand beside the sword that was tucked into her saddle. "These prisoners are coming to the palace," she informed the kneeling guardsmen.

"My lady, this is highly inappropriate. Surely you will not believe the words of these thieves over loyal men to the realm."

"First of all, it's Your Highness, not my lady and second, even loyal men can be in the wrong, when given orders by a corrupt lord. Now…" She turned to him. The guard eyed Mary's companions as though he were thinking of doing something stupid. "You are surrounded by the top ranking members of both Kale and Koloso, and to raise a sword against your reigning sovereign is an act of treason. Do you really want to engage in a fight you have no hope of winning?"

A moment of silence passed before the guard finally hung his head. "You're wrong about what is going on here, princess. But we will come quietly regardless."

"We shall see," Mary replied before re-mounting her golden hose. The group rode in silence to the palace gates, which opened at Kyle's command. "See these men get refreshments," she instructed Kyle. "Then we shall see about getting to the bottom of this. And, by the way," she turned to Brandan, "I'm sorry about running off. It was not my intention."

"There is no need to explain, princess," he replied with a slight nod before turning to see to the men. A few hours later, Mary found herself seated in the throne room with Kyle listening attentively as Rob and Cal described the most recent actions of the corrupt Usqubian lord. When they were finished, she called Lord Chiro to her side. After repeating the brothers' stories, she asked the Kolosian lord, "Is it true?"

Chiro met her gaze with a grave expression. "I know not of the specifics, my lady. Though what I can say is that the king had a tendency to allow some of his more 'favored' lords to rule their given realms as they saw fit, and often found ways to exclude the defendants from their ways."

"And the Lord of Usqub?"

"Would be among those 'favored,' Your Highness."

"I believe it is time we pay a visit to this Lord." Her eyes trailed to Kyle's. "This type of 'favored' behavior will be tolerated no further."

"As you wish," Kyle replied. "Shall I assemble a team?"

"Yes," she nodded. "We shall ride out as soon as a team is in place."

"Your Highness," Chiro cut in. "Is it wise for you to ride yourself?"

She turned her eyes back to the older man. "I plan to make an example of this man, my lord. I can't do that from behind palace doors." She turned back to Kyle. "Have Lady Rebecca assemble a group of defendants to ride with us in addition to your team."

Kyle turned and left the room at a brisk pace while Chiro took a moment to eye the young woman standing before him. "Pardon me, Your Highness, but…"

"I want them to know," Mary answered his thoughts. "I am doing this…no one else."

In response, Chiro gave another bow. "As you wish."

Two hours later, Mary sat astride her golden stallion, a few paces to the left of Lady Rebecca's golden and Lord Jiro's silver steeds. Kyle rode several steps behind her, just far enough to avoid the earth flung into the air by Sherwyn's thundering hooves. Farther back rode twelve additional defendants including Lord Callow in robes of brilliant red.

It was high noon on the second day when Mary's party arrived at the Province of Usqub under an immaculate violet sky. True to Rob and Cal's predictions, guards rode throughout the border of the province. However, at the sight of the royal entourage, they halted their patrols. "Have them join us," the princess ordered the Golden Defendant. "If they are with us, then they can't run and warn their lord."

Lady Rebecca nodded before issuing orders for the guards whose path they crossed to fall into place behind the royal escort. Then Lady Rebecca moved to the front of their assembled team riding fast as they eventually neared the town the two brothers had named as their home: Belliam.

Chapter VIII

◆⋅▻⋅✦⋅◅⋅◆

They did not enter immediately, instead pausing several miles outside of the small town. When the entire party had gathered, the princess dismounted from her golden stallion and pulled a long black cloak from her saddle bag. It closed at the neck with a small blue stone, completely hiding Mary's golden robes. Beside her, Brandan and Kyle followed suit, though both men also maneuvered their sliver blades to the outside of their black cloaks. When she glanced at Kyle he answered, "We must be able to reach them quickly if needed, and our silver blades are less noticeable than your golden." She nodded and left her own blade under the cloak, tied securely to her left hip. Then the three riders, along with several defendants, switched their golden mounts to the black ones that had been ridden by those of lesser rank and proceeded to enter the town. When they eventually reached a small inn, Mary turned to Lady Rebecca who rode by her side.

"Kyle, Brandan, and I will go in here." She motioned to her left. "The rest of you explore other parts of the town. I will see you back at the horses in one hour, if not before."

Lady Rebecca nodded before breaking off from the group. Mary pulled on the reins of the unfamiliar horse. Behind her, Kyle dismounted from his own steed and walked to her. He took the reins, holding her horse steady as the princess dismounted. After securing the horses to the wooden rails provided by the inn, Kyle turned back towards Mary and Brandan, and followed them into the small tavern.

The wooden porch attached to the front was badly in need of repair, sporting stains, holes, and splintered handrails beside the steps leading up to a swinging, saloon-style door. Kyle pushed the door open for the princess. As Mary stepped through, she turned and spoke softly. "I wish to speak with some of the locals and ensure we have the right story."

He nodded without speaking, so Mary turned and walked into the room beyond with the two Kolosians following closely behind her. The walls of the inn were dark with gray paint peeling at the corners of the building. The wooden floor creaked under their feet. Small tables lined both sides of the room and a long marble bar stood against the left wall. Mary walked to the bar, placing her hand upon the cold gray marble as an older woman with long brown hair and matching eyes moved to greet them. She wore a black, long-sleeved shirt and a long black skirt that shuffled as she moved about on the other side of the bar.

She gazed up at Mary and then to Kyle, who proceeded to order a round of drinks and placed several small pieces of silver into the bartender's hand. Mary then turned and gazed around the small room filled sparsely with different people at the small tables. A low murmur occupied the room with no one voice more distinguishable from another. "Mary," Kyle interrupted her observations. She turned and accepted the glass of clear liquid he offered before turning from the bar and moving to one of the small tables on the right side of the room. They settled into hard wooden chairs, seemingly ignored by the locals as the trio sipped on their drinks.

Mary watched the people at the bar as she drank, noting the comings and goings of the townsfolk until she finally rose to order another round of drinks. Kyle stood as well, but she shook her head. "I'm going to order more drinks; it's only a few paces away."

He looked at her uneasily before reluctantly nodding and retaking his seat. Mary walked back across the room and took a seat on a tall wooden stool before the marble bar. Beside her sat an older man with short gray hair and a beard of stubble. His face was alarmingly thin which highlighted his sharp chin and high cheekbones. Beside him sat a younger and equally thin man, with dark brown hair and olive skin. As she sat, the bartender approached the two men first. "Hey there, Brent," she addressed the elder of the two. "What can I get for ya?"

"Some broth for my friend," Brent replied, pulling a piece of silver from his left pocket.

"No," the younger man replied. "I can't let you do that."

"Yes, you can, Thomas." Thomas parted his lips to argue when Brent interrupted. "You have three children to feed and I know that you skipped dinner last night. You're no good to them if you're too starved to work. Save your silver for the kids." He then placed a piece of silver onto the edge of the bar, which the woman took before turning to Mary, who proceeded to order another round for herself and the two Kolosians. To her surprise, Brent turned to her. "It's a fortunate person indeed who can afford a drink in these times."

Mary glanced up, startled at being addressed directly. She then reached into the pocket of her black outer robe and switched from silver to gold.

When the innkeeper brought her drink, she slid the golden piece into the woman's hand discretely and nodded toward the two men seated beside her. "One for those two as well."

Startled at the golden piece, the innkeeper nodded and went to fetch more of the clear alcoholic liquid for the men in question. When the drinks were placed before them, they turned towards her. "Thank you, ma'am," Brent said.

"Awfully generous of you," added Thomas.

"No problem," she replied, turning in her seat to better face the two men. "It seems like hard times in these parts."

"Could say that again," the younger of the two addressed her.

"It wasn't always like this," Brent replied, shifting in his seat as he took a deep sip of the offered drink. "Ah, I can't tell you how much I have missed the taste of a good drink."

"What happened to bring such," she searched for the word, "rough times?"

"Well you see…"

"Quiet Brent," Thomas cautioned. "You know what will happen if they hear you running your mouth off again."

"Again?" Mary asked.

Thomas leaned closer across the bar. "Last time someone ran their mouth off, they were whipped in the square for questioning their *rightful*," he made the word sound like something sour, "sovereigns."

Mary leaned in even closer. "Whipped? Does this happen a lot?" Brent nodded while Thomas looked on in silence. "What else?"

"They…"

"Quiet!" Thomas hissed.

Brent turned back to Thomas. "Do you think I care what they do to me? What, exactly, do I have left for them to take from me?" He turned back to Mary. "You must forgive my nephew. It has not been easy on him."

"Look," Thomas interrupted. "I do not know where you are from, or how you got through the guards at the borders, but it would be best if you leave as soon as possible." He stood from his chair and added, "Thank you for the drink," before turning and walking towards the wooden doors, leaving the tavern.

Brent turned to Mary and again said, "It wasn't always like this. When the temples held power and the defendants protected the land, things were better." He leaned in very close and whispered for Mary's ears alone. "It was when power was taken away from the temples and given over to these so-called lords, when the real trouble began." He leaned back and his voice began to increase in volume. "When the temples were in power, people prospered. They were safe. The defendants protected them. They didn't rob the people blind, allowing them to starve while the lords sit on their piles of gold."

"Quiet!" the bartender's harsh voice cut through the elderly man's rant. "We don't want any trouble here."

"Trouble? We've had nothing but trouble for years."

"Please," the woman cautioned. "Someone will hear you."

"Do you think I care?"

"Brent, please!"

Kyle stood from his table, crossing the room in long strides to arrive at Mary's side. "Is everything okay?" he asked, his hand moving to rest on the top of his silver blade.

"No!" the man answered, anger radiating through his voice. "Nothing is okay, can't you see that? It hasn't been okay since King Darek took the throne!"

Mary glanced at Kyle, whose hand had tightened on his sword. "It's okay," she told the silver Kolosian, moving her hand to lightly touch his before turning back to the old man, whose eyes slid over Kyle's tall form.

Kyle returned his voice to a whisper as he asked, "The question is, Your Highness. What are you going to do about what is happening here?" He stepped even closer to Mary, placing his sheathed blade within an easy sweep of the elderly man.

"Kyle." Mary's voice was sharper than she had meant for it to be. The sound of creaking wood drew her attention to the wooden doors of the inn, where three men garbed in the deep purple robes of the Usqubian Guard entered the room and walked towards the bar.

"Is there some trouble here?" one of them asked.

"No," the barkeeper replied. "No trouble."

The man ignored her and turned his eyes on the older man. Kyle stepped behind Mary, hiding his blade from view.

Mary turned to the guardsman with a smile. "We were just talking." She tried to sound as friendly as possible.

"Ranting is probably more like it," the guard replied, motioning to Brent. "We've had trouble with this one before. But you...I don't think I've ever seen you before."

Mary drew a slow breath as the guard took a step closer, causing Kyle to place a hand firmly upon her shoulder. The guard stopped at Kyle's movement.

Across the room, Brandan stood from his table, unsure if he should move closer. Mary didn't dare draw the guard's attention to him. Instead, she offered another smile. "Honestly, we were only talking. Surely that is no crime in the Kingdom of Kale? If my friend disturbed someone, I apologize. We will try to speak more softly from now on."

The lead guard turned his dark brown eyes upon Kyle and took another small step towards where the princess was seated. "That's close enough," Kyle informed him.

"Who are you?" the guard inquired.

"No one of consequence, unless you continue to walk toward my lady."

"And if I do?"

"You don't want to do that," Mary responded. "Look." She motioned towards Brent. "My friend had a little too much to drink. I am going to take him home." She kept her practiced smile in place. "No harm done."

"If he can afford his drink, then I assume he can also afford to pay his dues to the guard," the man responded. "Or would it be your protector who could afford it?"

"By all means. I would be happy to buy you a drink, if you wish."

He grabbed the old man roughly by the arm. The elderly man gave a loud grunt as he was jerked forward and forced to move between the other two men. "This man has caused trouble before. He will be forced to pay accordingly." He paused, eying the princess. "Unless, of course, you would rather pay for him?"

Still seated on the wooden stool, Mary leaned away from the guard, pressing her back against Kyle's chest. She slid her right hand to her left, wishing she had not decided to keep her blade concealed under the thick black robe. "That man has done nothing wrong." She fought to keep the tension from her voice. "Under Kalian law, you have no reason or right to restrain him."

"And yet, under Usqubian law, I have every right."

Mary turned in her stool towards the bar and picked up her drink with her left hand. She used the cover of Kyle's body to slide the edge of her black robe up, her hand clasping the edge of her golden blade. She placed the drink back onto the marble bar and looked at the guard with a sideways glance. "Those words border on treason to the realm." Her voice was low, harsh.

The guard leaned forward again, towering over Mary in her seated position.

"Close enough." This time, there was no mistaking the threat in Kyle's voice.

"You're threatening a knight of the Usbqubian Guard?"

"Not if you keep your distance."

Mary looked up in a sideways glance at the older man. "Let him go. I'll buy you and your men a round of drinks. Then we can all be on our way."

The guard turned back to where his companions were holding the old man. "Take him to a cell. A few nights should remind him of his proper place." Then, the guard reached a hand toward the right side of Mary's face. She closed her eyes as his fingertips made contact with her skin, tracing a line from her cheek before grasping her chin, lifting her face to meet his eyes. For a moment, she met his gaze, then brought up her arm, her golden sword clutched tightly in her right hand. The blade sailed forward in a sharp movement, slicing deeply into the guard's forearm, though not completely through.

That came moments later, as Kyle's own silver blade slid down, clashing against her gold as the blades met in the center of the man's arm. Blood splattered Mary's face as the arm fell onto her black robe before sliding to the floor. Blood raced from the stump that remained. Mary stood, her blade clutched tightly in her hand as she stepped back to stand beside Kyle. From across the room, Brandan had used the distraction of the man's severed arm to race across the room and was suddenly standing on the opposite side of Kyle.

Moving slowly, the other two members of the Usbqubian Guard raised their own blades and moved towards the three champions. Mary stared calmly as a blade came down on her right side. She lifted her sword to block the movement while Kyle lunged forward at a low angle, sliding the tip of his blade to the man's stomach. The guard froze and Mary removed the man's sword from his hands.

Meanwhile, Brandan had stepped forward to meet the second challenger. The fight was over in moments as Brandan sidestepped his opponent's movement and brought his silver blade to the guard's throat. Both men froze while their companion lay on the ground, the blood racing from his body, pooling on the floor beneath him. Mary gazed down and for one moment, saw Marcus instead of the nameless guard lying in the pool of blood. She shook her head to clear the vision and then stepped back, moving to Brandon's side and taking his opponent's blade. She tossed the swords behind the bar and turned to Brandan. "Go find Lady Rebecca. Send her here immediately."

Brandan nodded and moved swiftly from the room while Mary turned her attention back to Brent. "Are you okay?"

"Yes, my lady," he replied. "Thanks to you and your fellow defendants."

Not bothering to deny it, Mary turned back to the guards. "Your companion is going to die without medical attention. I suggest you go get help."

"Defendant?" said the other. Mary pulled the black cloak from her shoulders, revealing the golden robes of Kale to the astonished crowd surrounding her. "You are not the Golden Defendant," the man said in confusion.

A second later, Lady Rebecca entered from the opposite side of the room with two defendants by her side. "Princess," Rebecca addressed her. "Are you all right?"

Mary nodded in her direction. "Send someone for help. This man needs a healer."

One of the defendants dressed in blue moved back towards the door and Mary motioned to one of the Usbuquian Guards. "Go with him."

The other guard knelt down to his companion. "Here." Mary handed him the robe she had been wearing previously. "Use the cloth to bind the wound." She then turned to the woman who stood in silence behind the bar. "My apologies. This was not my intention."

"Of course, my lady," the woman replied.

Mary walked towards the wooden door, falling into step behind Lady Rebecca as they emerged into the sunlight. "I sent Brandan for the rest of our party," the princess informed the Golden Defendant.

"Yes," Rebecca replied. "They should be here momentarily."

As the students and defendants stood outside the inn, more guardsmen appeared, but froze at the sight of the golden robes. Mary watched the group uneasily, then caught the glisten of brightly colored robes coming towards them. The royal entourage arrived, riding through the gathered crowd, surrounding the princess. Brandan rode forward, pulling Sherwyn behind him, and handed the reins to Mary, who mounted her golden stallion in a single stride.

As she pulled up on the familiar golden reins, she turned to address the crowd of guards and peasants. "I am Princess Mariana," she addressed them. "The golden student of the Temple of Kale and acting queen of the realm. And she," Mary motioned beside her, "is Lady Rebecca, the Golden Defendant. The Lord of Usqub will pay for what he has done here; you have my word." With that, she touched the side of Sherwyn's neck and the party rode off into the distance, Lady Rebecca once again taking the lead.

As they raced from the village and into the fields, the old man who Mary had saved stepped down the old wooden steps, catching the last gleam of her golden robes billowing in the light of Kale's three suns. He then proceeded to walk towards the south side of the small village, past the grassy blue fields to where the ground fell into the shadows of the tall, red trees that marked the beginning of the forest beyond.

Once he reached the trees, Brent took an old footpath through a seemingly tranquil forest. Yet as the shadows began to lengthen, the forest grew quiet. No animals raced along the underbrush. No birds fluttered through the tall trees. Despite this, he continued down the long path until the smooth dirt beneath his feet turned to blue grass and the trail vanished to all those who did not know its ancient path.

When he finally reached the shallow stream he had known so well as a child, he paused, kneeing down to drink from the cool, rushing water. When he looked up, he found himself staring into the reflective, catlike eyes of the wraith. Even with the river between them, the wolf-like creature's wild black fur stood in contrast to its sleek body Its razor sharp teeth were so large that they were visible from the side of its mouth even when his lips were fully closed. Brent's heart jumped to the back of his throat as he raised himself from the riverbank and took an inadvertent step back despite the river separating them. The creature gave a low growl from the back of its throat. Brent froze.

"You did well," hissed the wraith, shattering the silence of the dark forest.

"I did not realize she would be so…young." Brent managed to draw enough breath to reply.

"She is of age for my purposes."

"Yes," he replied sadly. "I suppose that is true. But to imagine one like her…someone who would risk herself to help an old man like me." He shook his head. "I guess it does not matter what she did, does it, my lord?"

"No," the wraith replied. "The fate of the twins is sealed before they are born."

The man looked solemnly at the dark creature. "I came for my reward."

"Yes." The wraith eyed him in silence for several moments and then took a step, leaping over the stream in a single bound. He landed squarely upon the man's chest, extending his claws, shredding his skin and tearing his lungs with deadly precision. "Your reward," the wraith growled. "Is to not live to see the horrors that come next." Then the wraith vanished, removing its claws from the dying man as the stream ran red with his blood.

Chapter IX

"That can't be right," Princess Ameria spoke aloud as she read through the old parchment yet again.

"What is it?" Breeze, the silver puppy of Koloso asked. He was covered with black fur with the exception of his white back paws and tail. "What did you find?"

"The archives at the Temple of Kale state that a man named Lord Kirkin was the silver student of Koloso the year after Lord Jiro. But I had never heard of a Lord Kirkin, so I decided to check the Kolosian records. Look here." Ameria stretched the previously rolled parchment flat against the wooden table, which stood in the center of the temple archives room. It was a large room, lined with tall shelves of books. In its center lay a spiral staircase that wound its way around the various levels of shelves which housed both coiled scrolls, such as the one she was reviewing, and thick bound books of leather, covered by layers of dust.

Ameria pointed to the line of parchment which listed the names of all the students to have served in the temple from the most current team all the way back to the time of Kale himself. Listed among them were Lord Rath and Lady Cerik, who had prevented an uprising in the Province of Flos nearly three hundred years before she was born. Lord Sherio, who was thought to be the longest serving Golden Defendant in history. Lord Lukas, Kyle's great-great-grandfather and, of course, Master Jiro and Princess Annabelle.

However, it was the following entry which drew her attention. "There are only nine names," she said to Breeze in confusion.

"What do you mean?" Breeze asked, jumping onto a chair beside the table to glance over her papers. After a moment, the puppy looked up and said, "Golden student Angelia?" He tilted his head to the right. "I have never heard of a Lady Angelia."

"Nor have I," Ameria replied. "I wonder if she died in service to the realm?" Breeze made no reply, so she continued. "Put that aside for now.

Look." She pointed again to the list of names. "Here's gold and red." She returned her gaze to Breeze's dark eyes. "But silver is missing."

"Do you think someone forgot to include... No." Breeze shook his head. "That makes no sense."

"Unless someone doesn't want anyone to know who the silver student was."

They stared at each other for several moments. "The only ones with the power to alter these documents," Breeze began.

"Are the temple masters."

"Or the high priest himself."

Chapter X

❖

The Lord of Usqub lived at the top of a low hill covered with bright blue grass and sparsely placed trees sprouting leaves of deep purple and bright reds. One of the largest rivers in the kingdom ran along the edge of the hill, smaller only than the powerful water that ran the length of the Rainbow and Dark Mountains. Though not as grand as any temple or palace, the manor the Usqubian Lord called home was still an impressive site. It was a fifteen room mansion with towering glass doors, vaulted ceilings and spiraling pillars which held it up from the ground below. It was surrounded by a tall, black fence that encircled the lord's lands, both protecting those within and preventing outsiders from entering unannounced.

As the royal entourage approached the lord's manor, Lady Rebecca pulled back on her reins. Motioning for Lord Callow to ride ahead, the Golden Defendant moved her horse behind Mary's, flanking the princess' right with Kyle on her left. When the two riders reached the black gate, they called out: "Open in the name of the Crown Princess and the Golden Defendant!"

The gates opened moments later and the riders advanced. Rushing through the blue grass, they soon reached the front of the tall manor which the Usqubian lord called home. As they approached the building, several guardsmen exited the house wearing dark purple robes. "What is going on here?" one of the men asked, squinting against the light of the three suns hanging high in the purple Kalian sky.

Members of the royal escort spread out in a large half circle while Mary and Rebecca moved their golden stallions several paces ahead of the others, Kyle deferring to those of higher rank. Lord Callow, the Red Defendant, addressed the man who spoke. "The Golden Defendant and the Crown Princess."

The Usqubian men gazed at the gathered riders in a daze and began to kneel. Mary turned to the guard who had spoken. "We are here to see your lord. You will have him brought here immediately."

Moments later, the Lord of Usqub stepped into the sunlight, emerging from the tall glass doors of the manor. He took several steps, gazing through the gathered riders before finally settling upon the golden-clad women in its center. "What in the..." He paused, then slipped down to one knee beside his men. "My ladies," he addressed them. "Forgive me. I had not received news of your visit."

He was a stout man with short gray hair and a stubbly beard. His skin was a few shades darker than Mary's, marking his mixed heritage. He wore purple robes of state that matched those of his men.

"Rise, Lord Garrith," Mary addressed him.

"My princess," he replied rising to his feet. "Forgive me, my lady. What has happened? I received no word of your approach."

"Nor would you have. We rode at great haste from the palace."

"What has happened?" he asked again, eyeing the accompanying riders. "Has there been another threat to the realm?"

Mary drew a deep breath and exhaled slowly. "Yes, my lord. In a manner of speaking, I would say a grave threat indeed."

He bowed his head. "I am at your service, my lady."

"Are you?" Mary asked. "Are you truly?"

Garrith glanced up apprehensively. "But of course, my lady."

"And do you seek to loyally uphold the laws of Kale as well? To protect this crown, these lands, and the people upon them from all that would threaten them?"

"Of course, Your Highness. I strive always to protect the kingdom... your kingdom."

"And those men at the border?" Mary pulled on Sherwyn's reins, causing the horse to take a step forward. "Were those men at the border protecting the people as well?" Her voice sounded cold.

"The...the men?"

"Yes," Rebecca replied. "The ones at the border." She motioned behind her to where two of the lord's own men sat astride a pair of black horses. "These two were kind enough to join our entourage as we rode through the kingdom." The Golden Defendant's voice matched the coldness of Mary's. "The stories they have told have been rather...treacherous."

Lord Garrith's eyes narrowed and his head tilted slightly to the right. "The men at the border guard the province from invaders, my lady. If they have neglected this duty, it is the first I am hearing of it."

"From what kind of threats?" the Golden Defendant inquired.

"She means," Kyle moved his silver mount to stand beside Mary's gold, "do your men fight to keep invaders from entering the realm or to prevent your people from escaping it?"

"Escaping it?" the Lord stammered. "Why would they wish to escape, my lord? I have no idea."

"Choose your words carefully," Lady Rebecca spoke from her place beside Mary, the hooves of her golden stallion pawing the ground excitedly. "It is a crime to lie to a Lord of Koloso and treason to lie to a Lady of Kale."

"Koloso," Lord Garrith said, shifting his gaze to Kyle's silver robes. "That would make you Lord Chiro's son?"

"Yes," Kyle replied dryly.

"I don't understand," Garrith finally said. "What is going on here?"

Mary drew a deep breath and turned her emerald eyes upon the Usqubian lord. "Lord Garrith of Usqub," she addressed him formally. "By the power granted to me by the Gods of Kale and as your acting queen, princess, and presiding Master of the Kalian Temples, I hereby charge you with treason against to the realm."

"Treason!" Garrith stuttered. "I have never been anything but loyal to the crown."

"I charge you with the oppression of your people, theft of their goods and property, and the unjustified murder of those who attempted to speak against the actions of both you and those most loyal."

He gaped up at the young woman for several moments before finally trying to speak. "My princess," he began. "I assure you if something in my province is amiss, this is the first I am hearing of it. I am no traitor, my lady. I have no idea what you think I have done, or from where you have heard these vicious lies."

"I saw the villages," Mary replied. "I watched an old man buy his nephew a bowl of soup so his children would not starve. I watched your men abusing an elderly man and the brutality that was afflicted when someone tried to reason with them. The very idea that this is happening in my kingdom is sickening! And here you are, living in your mansion, plump on the seeds of their starvation!" She shook her head, Sherwyn beginning to prance in place at the sound of her raised voice.

"My lady, I do not know what you are…I had no idea."

"Then you do not deserve to be a lord!"

"Your uncle," he began.

"Is no longer among the living," she replied coldly, lowering the volume of her voice. "If you truly did not know what was happening in your own province then you are unfit to be its lord. If you did know, then you have wronged the very people you swore to protect. Either way, you have broken the oaths which every lord takes upon being bequeathed such an esteemed position in the realm."

Sherwyn still moved nervously and Mary pulled on the reins, moving the stallion into a tight circle before turning back to face the confounded lord. "You will be taken into custody by the defendants and escorted to the palace towers, there to be held until such a time that I feel you have paid for your crimes." She drew a deep breath. "In addition to your imprisonment, I also hereby strip you of your lordly title and revoke all power and privileges that come with it from both you and all your heirs to follow."

"But, my lady! My family!"

"Your family," Mary replied, "shall learn to live in the poverty you have seen fit to bestow upon others for so long."

"Please." The lord took several steps closer to the princess, falling to his knees before her in the grass. "Please my lady. Do not do this, punish me if you will but not my family."

Mary looked at him with a heart free of sympathy.

"My grandchildren."

"Yes," Mary replied. "Terry and Brad, aged four and five." Mary glanced toward Lady Rebecca, who remained motionless upon her golden steed, deferring completely to the princess. "Your grandchildren," she addressed the former lord. "They will be taken separately to the Temples of Bellum and Occidere, to be trained in the ways of the temple Gods. They will spend their lives in service to the realm which you have betrayed, in hopes of one day regaining the honor that you have taken from them on this day."

Mary turned to the men kneeling along the edge of the large house. "Remove your outer robes," she commanded the Usqubian Guard. They hesitated only briefly before rising to their feet and pulling the purple cloth of their outer robes from their bodies and tossing them to the ground. She then turned to Kyle. "Evacuate the house. Then, burn it to the ground."

"And the men, my lady?"

"If they are of the temples, they can be re-assigned by their masters. If they are not..." Mary drew a short breath. "Then they can join their former masters in the same poverty they helped to create."

Kyle nodded and moved to carry out the princess' orders. A half hour later, he watched in silence as a fire was lit, and blue flames leaped to devour the ancestral home of the Lord of Usqub, black smoke rising through the air, forming a cloud so large that it momentarily blocked the light of the Kalian suns.

As the flames reached higher, Mary moved her golden stallion away from the house before turning to face the surrounding crowd. Mary cleared her throat and raised her voice so all could hear. "I hereby declare this land to lie under the sole guardianship of the Temple Masters of Bellum and Occidere. All issues of the Province of Usqub will be overseen by the temples, and the temples alone." She glanced back to gaze at the fire burning behind her before adding, "These lands will be strangers to the Gods no longer."

Chapter XI

Two men stood across a grassy field as the smell of smoke filled the air. One stood in robes of silver, his hand clasped tightly on the hilt of a silver blade lodged in an elaborate matching sheath at his side. His hair was the color of sunshine and his eyes were as blue as Kyle's were green.

Across from him stood another man, whose hand rested upon the hilt of his own blade. His golden robes shimmered in the fading light as the last of the Kalian suns began to lower itself from the sky. His hair was black and his eyes were the same emerald green found so frequently within the Kalian bloodline. Behind each of the men stood a long line of warriors, garbed in various temple robes. They sat astride horses of multiple colors, each horse matching the robes of their riders. A fire raged in the distance, a red tinge tipping the edge of yellow flames as they danced along the trees of a small forest in the distance.

The two men stood starting at each other across the field before walking towards its center. "My Lord," the one in silver spoke to the golden warrior. "I don't understand. What has happened?"

"Come," the man in gold said to the silver with a smile. "I will show you."

The silver warrior stepped forth as the man in gold reached out his arm and placed it upon the silver man's shoulders. Then, faster than eyes could follow, a golden blade was drawn. Blood spewed forth, tainting the air with a crimson touch.

"No!" Kyle shouted as he rose from the thick blankets surrounding him. He drew a deep breath, attempting to shake off the effects of the dream. It was the same dream he'd had almost every night since the moment Marcus had died.

He climbed from the bed and pulled his silver Kolosian robes around his tall frame before lighting a candle by the side of the bed. The temple of Bellum had been created deep inside a rocky wall in the low hills of Usqub. The walls were gray, flecked with white stones representing the color of the Bellum temple, where the royal entourage had stopped for the night on their way back to the palace.

Disturbed by the repetitiveness of the dream, he walked from the room into the dark hallways beyond, lit by white torchlight. Several members of the royal guard patrolled the halls, including Brandan, who had been elected for the second half of the night watch.

"Kyle," the younger man addressed his longtime teammate. "I did not realize you would be…"

"Trouble sleeping," Kyle interrupted. "I assume all is quiet?"

Brandan nodded. "We're inside temple walls though, so I wouldn't expect it to be otherwise."

Kyle nodded. "I think I will walk around a bit anyhow."

"As you wish."

Kyle nodded towards Brandan before turning to continue his walk down the dimly lit corridor. The white flames danced across the gray walls before him, sliding between shadows as he stepped forward. When he finally reached the chamber where Mary lay, he dismissed the guards standing before the stone door. For several minutes, he stood still outside of Mary's chambers, watching the quiet hallway, wondering again about the men in his dream. *Who were they?* He searched his memory for any hint of where he might have seen them before.

As usual, he drew a blank. He shook his head before silently opening the large black door to the princess' chamber. He stepped inside quietly, closing the door behind him. His eyes slid across the room to Mary's sleeping form, lying on a small bed, covered in thick black blankets. She wore only a thin gown of gold, her upper back laid bare from where the covers had slipped, exposing her bare shoulders, her arm raised to slide under the black pillows beneath her.

He stepped to the side of the bed and pulled the blankets, covering her. As the tips of his fingers touched the edge of her long black hair, he found his hand lingering almost involuntarily. He raised his hand higher and gently brushed her hair back from her pale face. Her full lips parted as he ran his hand lightly over her cheek. "What do you dream, my lady?" he whispered into the darkness of the room.

Mary remained oblivious to his attentions and after several moments, he pulled back from his princess and returned to the tall stone door. Placing his back against the gray wall of her chamber, he rested his hand upon the hilt of his Kalian blade and listened to her steady breathing.

Chapter XII

Princess Ameria knocked on the tall, golden door. A few moments later, a voice called "Come in," from the other side. Ameria pulled the door open and entered the vast chambers of the High Priest Louis. She stepped toward the center of the room and knelt down to one knee, placing her arms straight on either side of her, her finger tips touching the ground, her golden robes flowing around her kneeling figure. Dressed in a thin sash of rainbow satin, the solid white puppy moved to meet her.

"Arise, princess," the high priest instructed. "What may I do for you, my lady?"

She stood from the thick rainbow carpet and gazed down upon the white puppy. "My lord, I have heard a number of disturbing things in the past few weeks. I was here hoping for some clarification."

"Disturbing, how, my lady?"

She inhaled sharply. "Who is Lord Nathan?"

"Lord…Nathan?"

"Yes," Ameria replied. "Nathan. A former defendant, if the story I was told is to be believed and the father to the man who murdered Prince Eadmund and Master Leo. Who is he?"

"I do not believe this is a story that should concern you, my lady."

"What?" she asked in disbelief. "I believe it does. This man's sons killed members of the royal family, in vengeance for what was done to him."

The high priest glanced around the room, refusing to meet her gaze. "Lord Louis," she said firmly. "I need to know what is going on. Who is Nathan and why did his sons kill my father?"

The high priest gave a heavy sigh and raised his head to meet the sapphire blue eyes of the princess. "Lord Nathan," he admitted, "was the silver student of Koloso. He was among the finest to rise from the temples. Though, sadly for him, he had the misfortune of arising at the height of Leo's success. He was a year too young to qualify for the thirteenth tournament, and would have had to wait eleven years to compete. Thus, he never actually had a chance to compete in the final tournament." The high priest cleared his throat. "Three years after your father and Leo's famous fight, Nathan found himself as fourth in command of the Defendant Team while his partner, Angelia, was seventh. Behind Leo, your parents, and Master Jiro, of course."

"Angelia?" Ameria inquired. "Who is…"

"A former golden student of Koloso. The year after your mother." Ameria gave a slight nod as the high priest continued. "Leo had been the Golden Defendant for nearly five years when King Nicholas, your grandfather, died. Three months later, your uncle, King Darek, decided to break his betrothal to Lady Annabelle."

She nodded. "My mother has informed me on multiple occasions that she was originally meant to be the king's bride."

Louis nodded. "The kingdom was pushed to the brink of war at the king's betrayal of your other grandfather, Lord Rickard. He was furious and his alliance with the High Lord of Serenitas and Usqub meant that half the realm was threatening to rise against the crown." Louis inhaled deeply. "Meanwhile, the defendants found themselves in an awkward position, with the king having a marriage outside of the temple law they were sworn to defend."

Louis gestured towards a chair covered in satin cushions, streaked rainbow, in the order of the temple colors. "Have a seat, my lady. It's a long story."

Chapter XIII

24 Years Ago

"We had better put a stop to this," Jiro said to his long time teammate.

"Too late," Nathan replied.

"What do you mean?"

"A messenger has arrived. Usqub and Serenitas have invaded the boarders of Agnus. Maser Lester is attempting to smooth the situation. But I am assuming…"

"Nathan!" a feminine voice interrupted.

"Yes?" Nathaniel asked, turning to see his longtime partner walking towards him. Angelia stood several inches shorter than the two men. The silver mark of Koloso stood clearly against her pink robes and her long brown hair was gathered behind her in a tight braid. "Leo is asking for you," she nodded towards the men, "both of you."

The two men turned as one and walked down the hall towards a set of tall golden doors. They had gathered at the Kalian Temple at the call of the High Priest Julian. As the tall doors opened, the two men entered the room and knelt down to one knee, their red and yellow robes pooling around them as they entered a traditional Kalian bow.

In the center of the large room stood a group of defendants including Lord Leo and Prince Eadmund, garbed in robes of gold and silver, along with Lady Annabelle in bright red. A group was speaking to High Priest Julian, a puppy with jet black fur and pale green eyes. Raised at the Temple of Ziazan, Julian had been trained from birth to be a liaison between the temples and the realm of the Gods.

"Arise," Leo instructed his fellow defendants. "We would appreciate your council, my lords."

"Of course," Nathan replied, rising to his feet with practiced grace. "What is the situation?"

"The Lord of Usqub and Serenitas are moving in on Agnus. Lester is trying to calm the situation, but it is to little avail." Leo shook his head, tossing his short blond hair.

"Can't Lady Annabelle talk to him?" Jiro inquired, turning to the defendant in question. "I mean, he is your father."

Annabelle shook her head. "He is at the head of an army. There is no good way to reach him."

"What I need," Leo interrupted, "is to dispatch a small group to try and negotiate the matter, before things get more out of hand than they already are. The Lord of Turbamentum has been kind enough to offer additional men to accompany the team."

Nathan shook his head. "How can we be of assistance?"

"I want you to be on the team that I am sending. Try and reason with the lords."

"I will go," Annabelle said. "No matter what the king has done," her voice held a touch of bitterness, "war between the high lords cannot be the answer."

"I shall go as well," Eadmund stated.

"So will I," Nathan and Angelia said in unison.

"Good," Leo responded. "I, on the other hand, will go to the palace and attempt to assure the king that we are doing all within our power to resolve this situation without bloodshed." Leo motioned to where Jiro stood on his left. "I would like for you to accompany me."

"Of course," Jiro replied, nodding in Leo's general direction.

"Good." Leo's gaze slid across the room. "You should leave immediately. You will stay in Turbamentum tonight and be accompanied by his additional forces.

A half hour later, fifteen defendants rode out from the Kalian Temple, the high priest watching them vanish into the never clearing mists of the Rainbow Mountains on steeds of gold and silver, their defendant robes billowing behind them in the powerful Kalian winds.

Chapter XIV

24 Years Ago

THEY RODE THROUGH THE ROYAL grounds of Turbamentum where they were joined by members of his personal guard and several additional defendants who had ridden from the Temple of Desoto to join their teammates. Once there, they paused for the night, gladly accepting the hospitality of the Turbamentum Lord.

They rode out early the next morning. Kale's three suns filled the violet sky. They raced past the Temple of Mortem before reaching the Temple of Postrema by moonlight. Before they settled down, Eadmund, Annabelle, Nathan, and Angelia gathered in a conference room, sitting before a large, circular table. Once gathered, it was Angelia who spoke first. "So," she began, "do we have a plan or are we going to improvise?"

"According to our scouts," Nathan replied, "the Serenitas army is heading towards the Lord of Agnus' private domain. He has paused his army there, waiting to coordinate with the Lord of Usqub, who is riding in from the north. We have another intervention party gathered at the Temple of Critous, awaiting orders from either Lord Leo or Prince Eadmund."

"We are going to have them head towards the grounds of the Lord of Agnus. While we will ride out with the first sun and attempt to intercede and reason with the quelling lords."

"And if they cannot be reasoned with?" The question came from Nathan.

Eadmund drew a deep breath. "Let's hope for the sake of the kingdom, they can be."

A few minutes later the meeting was adjourned. Prince Eadmund walked down the long dark corridor, his silver robes shuffling softly. Several temple students had generously offered their rooms to the defendants, and the prince had been offered a private room on the east side of the temple. When Eadmund reached the tall silver door, he was surprised to see a young woman garbed in black defendant robes, the crimson mark of Desoto on her left breast. Her long brown hair hung loosely around her thin frame. Her skin was so pale it seemed almost translucent in the dark room.

"Lilian," Edward addressed the young woman.

"Eadmund," she replied.

"Light some candles."

Lilian moved to the side of a small bed. A few moments later, dim light flickered and danced across the small chamber as three small candles burst to life.

"I'm surprised to see you here," Eadmund addressed her. "I thought you would stay at the Temple of Desoto."

"Where it's safe?" she asked.

"To help train the students," he half sighed. "I was going to say to help train the students. They do have that big tournament coming up, after all."

"Their training is fine," she replied, the dancing flames revealing the silhouette of a smile. "It is the Kalian students you should be worried about."

Eadmund returned her smile and took several steps towards her. "Is that so?"

"Watch," she replied. "Desoto will come out on top."

Eadmund slipped his arms around the young woman and pulled her close for a long, passionate kiss. She gave a gentle laugh as he led her to the bed behind them and pulled her down with him. Her laughter intensified as she slid down, her body collapsing on top of his.

"As far as I am concerned, you can be on top anytime." Lilian pressed her lips to his again and then slid to Eadmund's side. He wrapped his arms around her as their black and silver robes blended with the dark blankets beneath them. Lilian turned enough to gaze into his green eyes.

"I missed you," she said sweetly.

"I missed you as well," the prince replied.

"Then what are you complaining about?"

Eadmund hugged her close. "Trying to keep you safe is all."

"Eadmund." Her voice was soft. "I'm a defendant, and besides, if I stayed home I wouldn't be the woman you fell in love with."

Eadmund kissed her again. "Well, at least I get to have you here with me." He nuzzled against her neck and breathed deeply. "So," he finally asked, "are you ever going to marry me?"

She gave a sigh and then said, "Soon."

"Why not now?"

"We have talked about this. I am not ready to be a princess yet. I am doing so much good on this team right now." She shook her head, her long hair sliding across the pillow beneath her. "I just want it to last a little longer."

"You can be a princess and a defendant, you know? The two don't have to be mutually exclusive."

"But once I am a princess, they will treat me differently. You know they will. And then they will start demanding children."

"No." Eadmund shook his head. "I am a prince, remember, not a king. The only children they are interested in are my brother's. His children will inherit the throne, not mine."

"I suppose you're right," Lilian said slyly. "Our children will be too busy winning gold for Desoto to bother with running the kingdom."

Eadmund moved his hand down, tickling her side until she squealed with laughter. "We'll see about that," he said, adding his laughter to her own.

The two emerged the following morning with the rising of the first sun. They rode north in a sea of swirling robes, the sun at their backs. It would take two days of hard riding to reach the army and fear was strong that they would not reach the location in time. They spent a night around a large fire under a starlit sky before again rising early. When they finally reached the line of soldiers standing on the edge of the Serenitas army, Nathan and Annabelle moved to the front of their riding party, their defendant robes waving in the wind behind them. A guard wearing a dark blue robe rode from among the looming soldiers to meet them halfway across the grassy blue field. Nathan pulled his mount to a stop and addressed the approaching guard. "The Silver Defendant, Prince Eadmund, is here to speak with the Lord of Serenitas."

"I don't believe the lord wants…" The guard sounded unsure as he answered the higher ranked lord.

Annabelle interrupted. "My father is not fool enough to reject the prince of the realm, and he cannot reject the Silver Defendant. Now step aside, Garrett."

The older man looked like he wanted to argue, but instead relented, motioning to the men standing behind him. "Make way for the Silver Defendant, and the Lady of Serenitas." He pulled his large, black horse to the side, allowing the defendants to surge towards the center of the camp.

Chapter XV

―・⊱・✧・⊰・―

Mary stood in the pouring rain. Her long black hair lay matted against her head, beads of water glistening on the edge of the dark strands as they slid onto the cloth covering her shoulders. Her drenched clothes clung to her skin as she knelt down in the wet blue grass. Her head was down, green eyes closed tightly, the harsh wind biting into her frozen skin.

"Mariana," the firm, masculine voice slid through her mind. "Mariana, look at me."

Mary raised her head against her will to find herself staring into Marcus' deep green eyes. His long silver robes stood dry despite the downpour. His eyes were full of sorrow and the many words fluttering in her mind died as she gazed into them.

"Look at me," Marcus said again. Blood ran down his body, sliding across the slick satin of his silver robes, falling like the rain across Mary's own. "You let them kill me, Mary. You let them kill me."

"Marcus, I..." The blood began to spread across the blue grass, sliding towards her, touching the edge of her golden robe. She tried to stand, but her body refused to respond. She watched, paralyzed, as the blood crept closer, the warm, wet liquid seeping through her thin robe to paint the pale skin beneath.

"Mariana!" His voice sounded unsteady. "Look at what they have done to me!"

"No!" Mary yelled as the cold wind began to blow harder around her. She fought to rise, but her body again refused to respond. The blood became a living thing, climbing up her arms as the rain continued to pour down upon her, sliding across her chest when Marcus leaned forward.

"Look at what you let them do to me!" His voice raced through the raging wind. He slowly reached out his left hand, covered with blood, and caressed her pale cheek. The warm blood was searing against her cold skin. She screamed, jerking back, away from his touch. She fell against the cold, wet grass as the slanted, catlike eyes of the wraith appeared in the corner of her vision.

"Death," he whispered.

A clout of thunder filled the air. She let out an ear-splitting scream.

"Mary!" Kyle's voice cut through her fear, pulling her from the nightmare. She jerked in a panic and attempted to climb from the bed. "Mary!" Kyle tried again. She fought harder, her nails slicing through the thin material of his silver robes and into the skin beneath.

He let out a low hiss, moving his hands to Mary's wrists, pressing her body down to the bed. "Mary, Mary, Mary."

"I have to save…I have to…I have…" Her breathing was ragged as she fought against Kyle's strong hands. Her body began to shake as she looked up into his eyes. He held her gaze for a moment, then eased his grip on her wrists. He leaned back, allowing Mary to sit up on the bed.

"You were dreaming, my lady."

Her breath was unsteady. Her eyes darted from Kyle to the far wall, then back to him. "I'm…"

"It's okay, my lady."

She fought to stop the tremors that ran up and down her body. She raised her arm, pressing the back of her hand against her lips and drew a series of deep, shaky breaths. He grabbed her free hand, sliding it into his own. She clung to his hand as she fought to regain her composure.

"I am here, my lady." Kyle swallowed hard and reached his other arm around her, pulling her gently until she lowered her hand and pressed her cheek against the silver cloth covering his broad chest. She did not cry, but merely leaned against him until her breathing began to steady. He ran his fingers through her long black hair, carefully avoiding contact with her pale skin.

"My lady," he said in a deep voice. "What can I do?"

Mary raised her head from his chest to gaze up into his eyes. She then leaned closer, pausing with her lips only a breath from his own. He cupped the side of her face as she closed her eyes, remaining perfectly still under his touch.

"Mariana."

She drew a long, slow breath and exhaled slowly. Then she opened her eyes, stood, and stepped forward in the candle-lit room. She took a heavy golden robe of wool from where it lay on the tall dresser. She unfolded the heavy garment and slipped it around her shoulders before closing it with a satin sash, eclipsing the thin gown beneath. She then pulled her long black hair from outside the robe and arranged it around her face. At last she turned back to Kyle, who had risen from the bed to stand several paces behind her.

She drew another breath. "The sun should begin to rise momentarily. Wake the others. We ride with the first of the sun's rays."

Chapter XVI

24 Years Ago

Prince Eadmund, Lady Annabelle, Lord Nathan, and Lady Angelia rode through the camp. Hundreds of large tents stood upon the blue grass, housing thousands of men who had risen to the call of the High Lord of Serenitas. Second in size only to Turbamentum, Serenitas was easily considered the most powerful of the Kalian provinces. Its ruler, Lord Riccard, was a powerful man and a former Golden Defendant. His tent stood near the center of the camp and as the riders approached, the high lord himself stepped out into the sunlight to greet them.

Lord Riccard was a tall man with deep blue eyes. His hair was more sliver than the sandy brown it had been in his youth. With a lineage as pure as the royal family's, his pale skin was covered by golden robes, the mark of Kale upon his chest. Lord Riccard stepped forward, a silver blade tucked against his side in a golden sheath. As the defendants reached the tent, they moved their horses side by side, forming a single line before the powerful lord.

Riccard gave a single nod in the defendant's direction before shifting to kneel in a traditional Kalian bow. "Your Royal Highness," he addressed the Crown Prince. "I wish I could say I was pleased to see you on this day."

"Yes," the prince replied. "These circumstances are most grave." Eadmund's horse began to prance nervously, and the prince dismounted from the saddle. "You may rise, Lord Riccard."

The older man stood as the other defendants followed the lead of their prince, dismounting from their respective steeds. Riccard allowed his eyes to survey the other riders, finally settling his gaze upon Annabelle. "Hello, daughter."

"Greetings, Father," she responded.

"I am surprised to see you, considering it is your honor I am defending."

"I can defend it fine on my own, Father. I never asked you to do such a thing."

"Well, apparently you can't," the lord replied sharply. "Or at least it would seem that you have failed, as you are here while the daughter of Agnus sits upon your throne."

"Father…"

"And you, Prince Eadmund," Riccard interrupted, shifting his gaze back to the prince. "I am surprised you are not at arms yourself. It is, after all, the temples you serve which the king has betrayed."

"My lord, while it is true that my brother has made a grave—"

"Have you come to join me, my prince?" Riccard stepped closer, giving Eadmund the full weight of his gaze. "Join our cause. I will make you a king."

The air seemed to still at the lord's words, both parties staring at each other for several long moments. It was Annabelle who finally broke the silence. "Father, do be serious."

"I am serious, daughter." His voice was firm. "I will make him a king. Place a Kalian back on the throne where he belongs. Bring an end to this rift between the temples and the crown." He turned back to Annabelle. "All he has to do, is say yes."

Chapter XVII

Princess Mariana rode past the golden gates of the palace, racing towards the entrance without pause or concern for the party that rode behind her. As she approached the front entrance to the palace, she found Lord Chiro awaiting her on the white marble steps with the sleeves of his silver robes blowing in the wind. As she rode closer, Chiro knelt down to one knee in a traditional Kalian bow while those around him moved to follow suit. All three of the kingdom's suns filled the violet sky, causing the marble and glass to shimmer in the brilliant light.

Mariana reached the bottom of the marble steps, pulling sharply on Sherwyn's reins to bring the golden horse to a complete stop. Behind her, Kyle and Lady Rebecca did the same. They were followed a few paces later by the rest of the princess' entourage. As she stopped, several men dressed in the deep crimson of the royal guard moved to assist their princess from her mount. Mary ignored them, leaving the saddle with practiced ease and ascended the white steps of the palace.

Mary greeted her advisor as she reached the top. "Arise," she addressed the High Lord of Turbantium before turning towards the woman kneeling at his side. The older woman's long brown hair hung loosely down her back in soft waves, covering her bright red robes which Mary knew would have the golden mark of Kale embroidered into the soft material. "Lady Laciety," she addressed the High Lady of Flos and former Red Defendant. Lady Laciety stood from her kneeling position and turned her brown eyes upon Mary.

"Greetings, Princess Mariana."

"The same to you, Lady Laciety," Mary replied. "I am glad to see you here."

"I was honored to receive an invitation of a place upon your royal council, Your Highness."

"Please," Mary addressed her, motioning towards the tall doors, "accompany me inside?"

Lady Laciety nodded in consent and the two women stepped through the doors of the palace, opened wide by guards. They walked down the crimson carpets through several long corridors in silence, followed by Chiro and several other members of the party Mary had arrived with. When they finally reached the large, black door to the throne room, Lady Laciety turned to the princess. "Your Highness," she began. "I would like to offer my condolences on the death of both your father and partner. My son spoke fondly of Lord Marcus, and I served with your father through many a battle in our youth. Both will be sorely missed for many years to come."

"As is your son, my lady." Mary inhaled. "Jace was one of the best I have ever had the privilege to stand beside." She paused to draw a deep breath. "I apologize, my lady, for not coming to see you in person after his funeral."

"No apologies needed, Princess Mariana. You attended the funeral and honored my son. That is all that matters."

Mary gave a single nod before leading the party through the tall, black doors and into the room beyond. The room was a vast, open space with a floor of silver. Two thrones stood at the top of a long series of marble stairs. Behind the throne stood a wall of solid glass that twisted the light filtering in from Kale's three suns in a prismatic array of color, which danced across the silver floor in a blinding flurry of brilliant light.

Mary squinted against the brilliance of the sunlight while she spoke to the men and women who stood behind her. "I need a private word with Lord Chiro, before the rest of you join us." The room cleared as Mary walked to the bottom of the steps leading to the thrones, her black heels echoing across the silver marble. She found her gaze sliding along the solid glass wall, which stood absent of any sign of the fight she had endured with her sister the night Marcus had died.

A shift in the clouds caused the light to become even brighter, forcing Mary to close her eyes against its brilliance. She lowered her gaze towards the floor, listening to the retreating sounds of footsteps across the marble. When the room finally fell to silence, she opened her eyes to find the floor covered by a thin layer of blood. She stared down at the blood as it slid towards her, her mind reeling at the sight.

"My lady," Chiro's voice cut through her mind.

She took a startled step back, slipping on the slick marble. She stumbled, managing to recover in time to keep from colliding with the floor.

"Princess Mariana," Chiro called out, grabbing her shoulder in an attempt to steady her. Mary blinked several times, fighting to clear her vision as the red floor turned back to silver.

"Sorry," Mary said in a less than steady voice.

"It is all right, Your Highness." Chiro's emerald eyes searched Mary's own. "My lady, we could do this at another time. You have had a long ride back from the temples, I am sure."

Mary looked at Chrio before asking, "Are they here?"

Chiro nodded. "Both Lord Vance of Periculum and Lord Harcort of Agnus have arrived at the palace, as you requested."

"It would be wrong to keep them waiting…would it not?"

"My lady," Chiro answered. "You are, for all intents and purposes, the queen and rightful heir to the throne. Lords wait upon you, princess. Not the other way around."

Mary felt her heart quicken at his words as she fumbled for a response. "I know that," she finally said. "I am…"

"No need to explain. I only wanted to ensure that you understand your new role." She found herself staring at the floor, avoiding his gaze as she thought of what to say. Chiro stepped closer to Mary and gently moved a hand towards her face, raising her gaze to his with a light touch. "Another thing, my lady; a queen lowers her eyes to no one."

Mary stared into Chiro's eyes for several moments before nodding. "I want this to be done sooner rather than later," she told him. "Send for the other members of the council." She turned, gazing up at the silver throne before beginning to ascend the marble steps. The sound of her heals slid across the room. "Then," she further instructed the high lord, "send for the Lords of Angus and Periculum. They are to wait outside until called upon."

When she reached the top of the steps, she turned back to Chiro who had stooped into a low bow. "As you command, Your Highness." Mary gave a wave of her hand before turning once again. She then drew a deep breath and exhaled before taking a seat upon her uncle's throne.

Chapter XVIII

24 Years Ago

Lady Annabelle sat in a large black tent beside her father, Riccard, the High Lord of Serenitas. They sat across from each other in wooden chairs padded with small black cushions. A pile of pillows and blankets sat in the far corner of the room, acting as a make-shift bed for the powerful lord. Prince Eadmund, along with the rest of the party sent by Lord Leo, had been moved into nearby tents, several of the king's men having agreed to give up their temporary lodgings upon the arrival of the defendants.

Annabelle attempted to make herself comfortable, adjusting the black pillows to better eclipse the hard wooden chair. She finally gave up, breathing a small sigh before straightening her red robes and turning her attention upon the man seated beside her.

"Father," Annabelle addressed him. "What were you thinking? Offering to help the prince overthrow his own brother?"

"I was merely offering to help the prince fulfill the vows he took when he put on those defendant robes."

Annabelle shook her head. "How does starting a civil war help the prince to honor his vows?"

"Blood and Arms," Lord Riccard stated as though the term explained everything.

"Blood and Arms?" Annabelle replied with a quiet scoff. She shifted in her wooden chair.

"Yes," her father replied.

"You are starting a war over…Blood and Arms?"

Her father looked at her with steady eyes. "Is there a more ancient or sacred vow in all the realm?"

She resisted the urge to roll her eyes. "Father, Blood and Arms is an old tradition, I know. But surely it is not worth going to war over."

"On the contrary, daughter. It is not I who started this fight. Neither am I the one who broke the most sacred tradition that exists within the Kalian temples."

"Father," she tried again. "Blood and Arms is…"

"A timeless, scared law," Riccard stated. "That has protected this realm for a thousand years. The sacred union between the power of the temples and the blood that runs through the veins of every royal to ever sit upon the throne is a union which must never be broken. It is the tradition which appeases the Gods and maintains the delicate balance in this world. The king's dismissal of the oath of Blood and Arms is an action for which the entire kingdom shall pay."

"Father, don't these beliefs of which you speak not strike you as somewhat archaic?"

"Archaic?" Riccard repeated.

"Superstitious," Annabelle said curtly. "It is a superstitious story…" she shook her head. "You are a high lord of the most powerful province in the kingdom. Don't you think that this is…" She drew a deep breath. "You are starting a civil war over…superstition!"

"No." Riccard's voice was firm. "The king started this, Annabelle. Not I. He broke the oath of Blood and Arms. He dishonored our family. Then, he furthered the insult by choosing, for his bride, the daughter of a lesser house."

Annabelle again shifted in her small chair. "Father, if you are doing this for me, then it is a gesture that I both understand and appreciate. But a war that is going to split the kingdom? Pit brother against brother from the lowest of stations to the royal family itself? All for the sake of a personal slight and an old superstitious story? This fight cannot be worth the price that it will cost the people of this kingdom."

"There you go with the superstition again." It was Riccard's turn to shake his head. "You, of all people, should know better. When your great, great, great uncle, Prince Lorcol attempted to marry a bride not of the temples, he was killed…"

"Please, Father. Not another—"

"He was killed," Riccard interrupted, "the night before his wedding, along with seven other members of the Defendant Team and two additional members of the royal family. Meanwhile, his youngest brother, your great, great, great grandfather, Prince Febrem, went on to—"

"To become king and have both of his sons serve as Golden Defendants," she finished for him. "I know the stories, Father." She sighed. "But what I don't understand is what Grandfather Febrem has to do with the current king taking a new bride."

"It was the oath," her father replied. "Your uncle Lorcol tried to break the oath, and the Gods killed him along with all those who attempted to support him in his marriage. It was their punishment for disobeying their sacred laws."

Annabelle gave another sigh. "Lorcol was killed by men from a neighboring province. Not the Gods, Father."

"It was the Gods!" he replied sharply. "They even sent their personal servants to carry out their execution."

She stared at him for several moments before saying, "You are saying that the Gods…the Gods themselves, were so angry about a marriage that they sent down their servants to kill the Defendant Team? Do you even begin to hear how crazy you are sounding right now?"

"Yes." The single word came out low and harsh.

"The messengers of the Gods," she repeated. "You know that they are only…myths. Old bedtime stories to scare young children."

Riccard leaned closer to the edge of his seat. "You know better than that, Annabelle Berhea."

Annabelle leaned back in her chair, her back straightening against the hard wood behind her. "Wraiths?" she finally asked. "You are saying that the wraiths…are real?"

Lord Riccard gave a slow, single nod, never removing his blue eyes from his daughter's. "They killed Prince Lorcol and his brothers, sparing only the youngest; the one betrothed to the golden student of Kale. The wraiths tore through the most powerful defendants in the land and bathed in their blood." He drew a slow breath. "That, my daughter, is the fate that befalls a prince who marries outside the sacred oath of Blood and Arms."

She stared at her father. She wanted to tell him his words were nonsense. That to fight a war over monsters in fairy tales was nothing short of ridiculous. Yet, she could not fight this nagging feeling. The conviction in her father's words frightened her, as though she were once again a child listening to old stories of the Gods and their vengeance.

She drew a deep breath, fighting through her sudden sense of fear. "Father," she finally addressed him. "I don't understand what is going on. You have always been one of the most rational lords of any realm. I mean…on one hand, you are talking about monsters in children's stories. Then on the other, you have called together this massive force of men, are putting your life, the lives of your men, and the fate of the very kingdom on the line. Your conviction cannot be doubted. But…" She paused for several moments, attempting to find words to continue. "Father, you cannot turn this kingdom to war."

"You may think that this army I have gathered will tear this kingdom apart, Annabelle. But let me assure you, if the king's marriage is allowed to stand, then there will be no need for myself or any other to take actions. The Gods will split it for us and when they come, no one on either side will escape unscathed."

"Father." Her voice was softer than she had wished for it to be. "The king…he married for love. Surely that cannot be a crime worth the cost of an entire kingdom."

"Love?" Her father spoke the word as though it were something foul. "No king in a thousand years has been allowed to marry merely for love." He leaned in, closing the distance between them to a mere whisper. "Being King is about duty, honor, justice. Placing the good of the kingdom before individual needs, personal gain, or private affection. It is for these things that heroes both proudly rise, and bravely fall. Wars have been fought and kingdoms have fallen in the name of love. But tell me daughter…what kingdom has ever been saved, in the name of love?"

Chapter XIX

Princess Mariana had asked five people to sit upon her Royal Council. Included were Lady Lacitey, High Lady of Flos; Lord Jiro, the Temple Master of Koloso; Lady Rebecca, the Golden Defendant; Lord Lester, the Temple Master of Critous and, of course, Lord Chiro, the High Lord of Turbamentum. Today, all five of these esteemed men and women of the realm were gathered together, kneeling at the foot of the throne before her.

At the top of the stairs, Mary sat uncomfortably in a silver throne. Watching the respective lords and ladies kneeling before her, she could not suppress the feeling that she might be out of her depth. Despite this, she addressed the gathered group. "Arise," she instructed. "I welcome you all to my court."

"We were honored at your request," Lord Chiro spoke as he rose from the ground in a shuffle of silver robes, an exact match to Lord Jiro's, who stood on his left.

"Yes," Lord Lester, dressed in temple robes of deep purple, stood on the right side of the room. "It is truly an honor, Your Highness."

Mary drew a deep breath. "I am glad to see each of you here, my lords and ladies. Not to cut the pleasantries, but I need to know if everyone here has been apprised of the recent events which took place during my journey to the Province of Usqub?"

"I have taken the liberty of informing the other council members, Your Highness," Lord Chiro informed her.

The Golden Defendant then took a step, her black heels striking the marble floor, causing the sound to echo across the glass chamber. "I believe that I can speak for this entire council when I say that we stand in complete support of your decisions. Your actions against Lord Garrith were both decisive and will send a clear warning to other lords of the realm that such corruption will be tolerated no longer."

Mary nodded at the Golden Defendant. "I thank you, Lady Rebecca." Mary shifted in her silver throne, unsure of how to broach the next subject.

Luckily, Chiro stepped in. "The princess and I," he addressed the others, "have been speaking of what steps must be taken in order to protect the people of the Kalian provinces from facing such corruption in the future." He gave a soft cough to clear his throat. "The princess has come to several important decisions, which she will share with you now." Chiro motioned towards Mary.

"Yes," Mary said. "My lords and ladies of Kale, a grave mistake was committed in the kingdom under the rule of the late King Darek. A mistake for which the people of these kingdoms have suffered greatly." She paused, unsure of the best way to continue.

Lady Laciety provided the path by asking, "What mistake, Your Highness?"

"The mistake, my Lady of Flos, was made when the late king, may he rest in peace, appointed men to several of the highest positions in the land who have never known what it means to stand at the service of the realm. Men who have never been held accountable to those over whose lives they have been granted the privilege of lording over." Mary straightened, pressing her back against the silver metal which was cold despite the abundance of sunlight filtering through the room. "Because of this, I have decided, in agreement with Lord Chiro, to strip both title and power from any and all high lords who were not raised within the temples."

Silence followed her statement, filtering down from the throne upon which she was seated and spreading to those who stood below. Minutes passed before the silence was finally broken by Lady Rebecca. "My princess," the Golden Defendant addressed Mary. "Am I to understand that you intend to carry out Lord Garrith's sentence upon any high lord not of the temples?"

"No." Mary shook her head. "I have no intention of imprisoning these men, or anyone for that matter, without just cause." She drew another breath. "But I also refuse to allow someone not of the temples to continue to hold power over the provinces for which I am now responsible."

"With all due respect," Lady Rebecca said. "You cannot possibly be considering punishing men of whose wrongdoing you have no proof. You cannot do such a thing."

Mary stared down intently into the dark eyes of Lady Rebecca, her heart seeming to beat far too fast. "With all due..." Mary paused, drawing a careful breath and tried again. "Lady Rebecca, what I do is for the good of the kingdom."

"But, my princess. You cannot punish these lords if they have done nothing to deserve a removal from their rank. You cannot punish them if they are innocent."

Mary found her gaze slipping to focus upon the floor. A part of her wondered if she should back down from her challenge, then Chiro's words floated through her mind. *A queen lowers her gaze to no one.* Mary raised her eyes from the floor and stood from the silver throne. "This is not about punishment, Lady Rebecca." Mary's voice came out surprisingly steady.

"Then what is it about?"

"Correcting the wrongs committed by my uncle."

"But if these lords have done nothing—"

"Exactly!" Mary interrupted. "They have done nothing! Nothing to deserve the positions they now hold. They serve neither the temples, the realm, nor the Gods. They were granted their positions without ever once having to serve the people they now rule. As such, they have no concept of either the honors they have been granted, or the duty to which every lord owes their people." She took several steps, pausing as she reached the top of the marble stairs.

"With all due respect to you, Lady Rebecca," Mary continued. "This is not a discussion. I am merely informing you of what is about to take place. I would prefer that you stand beside me as I carry out what I believe to be best for the kingdom." Mary paused, allowing her words to both rise and fade. "If any of you," she then addressed the room more broadly, "cannot do as I ask, I understand. However, please know this before you decide." She slowed her sentence. "If you cannot stand beside me now, you will never again be asked to sit upon this or any other council that is to be called upon in the future."

The Golden Defendant stared at Mary for a brief moment, then sank to the ground, her robes pooling around her body as she entered into a traditional Kalian bow. "Forgive me, Princess Mariana, if I came across as disrespectful. I am honored to be included among those asked to be on your council. I was merely attempting to ensure that you, as the acting queen, have considered all possibilities and options available to you. I will, of course, stand by whatever path you deem appropriate for both this council and the kingdom."

Mary nodded before turning to retake her seat upon the silver throne. "Arise, Lady Rebecca," she instructed the Golden Defendant. "Please ask Lord Vance and Lord Harcort to join us immediately." Rebecca stood in a swirl of golden robes. She walked across the marble floor and stepped outside of the large, black doors. A few minutes later she returned, with the two requested lords following closely behind her.

The High Lords of Periculum and Agnus wore matching black slacks and crisp, white long-sleeved shirts. Together, they walked to the center of the room, moving to the bottom of the steps and offered a bow. "Your Highness," the High Lord of Agnus addressed her.

"We are at your service," added the High Lord of Periculum.

Mary slid her eyes across the room until she finally met Lord Chiro's emerald gaze. Chiro gave the slightest of nods, a singular act of encouragement. Mary turned her attention back to the two lords kneeling before her. "Greetings Vance, High Lord of Periculum and Harcort, High Lord of Agnus.

"Greetings, Princess Mariana." Lord Vance was taller than Lord Harcort with short brown hair and matching eyes. "I was honored to receive your invitation to the palace."

"As was I," the blond haired lord, Harcort, spoke from beside him. "To what do we—"

"My Lords," Mary interrupted. "I have something to say to you both." She drew a short breath, fighting the urge to twist in the metal throne. "I would like to know, my lords, from what temple do you hail?"

"What?" Lord Vance paused as Mary awaited an answer. "I have never served in a temple, Your Highness."

"Nor have I," Lord Harcort added.

Mary gave a curt nod. "Have you ever entered any form of service to this realm?"

"Service," Vance responded. "I am not sure if I understand what you are asking, my lady."

"Let me show you," Mary replied, then turned her attention back to her chief royal advisor. "Lord Chiro, have you ever served the realm?"

"Yes, my Lady."

"How have you served the realm?"

"I served at the Temple of Koloso for fifteen years as a silver student, followed by two years at the Temple of Ziazan."

"And then?"

"I sat upon the Defendant Team for six years, serving two as the Silver Defendant, before retiring to the position of a high lord."

Mary nodded, then said, "Lord Jiro, have you ever served the realm?"

"Yes, my princess. Thirteen years as a student at the Temple of Koloso; one year at the Temple of Ziazan; ten years on the Defendant Team, four of which I held the rank of silver; and another fifteen years as a temple master, training the next generation of defendants."

"I," Lady Laciety said, "rose from the Temple of Kale and served as the Red Defendant for five years."

"Temple of Kale," Lady Rebecca stated. "Fifteen years on the Defendant Team."

Lord Lester rounded out the group. "I trained at the Temple of Desoto, but have served as the Temple Master of Critous for the last thirty years."

Mary shifted her gaze back to Lord Harcort and Lord Vance. "Again, I ask you, my lords: have you ever served the realm?"

It was Lord Vance who tried to answer. "I have been a high lord for…"

"That is ruling the realm, Lord Vance." Mary's voice was tight and controlled. "For the last time, the question is: have you ever served the realm?"

Mary stared at the two lords, allowing a profound silence to filter through the throne room. Then she said, "I take it, from your silence, that you have never served the realm. Would I be correct?" Neither responded, so she continued. "You have never served the realm. As such, it is the view and pronouncement of this," Mary gave a sweeping motion to those gathered, "royal council that you both are to be immediately stripped of the title high lord, for failure to have served the realm prior to your promotion to such an esteemed position within the Provinces of Kale."

It was Vance who responded first. "What?" He sounded shocked. "You are…stripping our titles?"

"Yes," Mary replied from her silver throne.

"You can't!" Harcort exclaimed. "We have done nothing to justify such dishonor."

"This is not about what you have done, my lords. But instead, about what you have not done." Mary paused for breath. "You have done nothing to deserve or earn the positions you hold. Because of this, you are, by decree of this royal council, hereby stripped of the rank of high lord. While you may keep the wealth you have accumulated during your time in this esteemed position, all future lands, wealth, and decrees shall be controlled by whomever this council deems fit to replace you."

"This is an outrage!" Vance exclaimed. The brown haired lord took several steps closer to the marble steps, causing Lord Jiro and Lady Rebecca to move, placing themselves between their princess and the disgraced lords.

"That is far enough," Lord Jiro instructed, his hand held tightly on the hilt of his silver blade, which hung loosely at his side.

Mary stood and walked to the edge of the stairs. "The decisions is final, my lords. You may see yourselves from this chamber, or I shall have these two," she motioned to the two warriors standing between them, "personally escort you from the palace grounds." More silence followed the proclamation, before the lords turned and walked from the throne room, the Golden Defendant at their heels. "Please see that they leave the palace." Mary gave the last instruction as the lords disappeared though the tall, black doors.

Chapter XX

———◆◦☆◦◆———

Princess Ameria rode through the mists of the Rainbow Mountains, the Silver and Red Defendants only a few paces to either side of her silver stallion. The never-lifting mist shrouded her, reflecting the murky light of the suns in an elaborate array of colors which danced on the edge of the wind, like fairies twirling around the riders, reflecting every color imaginable. Normally, Ameria enjoyed riding through these mountains more than any other path in the kingdom, however today she rode with a fierce purpose, barely noticing the beauty of the land surrounding her. She had been riding since the first of Kale's three suns had risen into the violet sky, riding over the wide blue grass blanketing the majestic mountain range which stood between the Temple of Kale and Ameria's destination: the estate of the High Lord of Serenitas.

It was nearly nightfall before the riding party reached their destination. A vast wall of silver surrounded the outskirts of the Serenitas estate. The only entrance stood on the north side of the grounds in the form of a large, black gate. As the gate came into view, she noted the large pillars of dark stone which stood on either side of the gate. On one pillar, in gold, stood the mark of Kale while on the other, the silver mark of Koloso glistened in the fading light.

As they approached the gates, Ameria pulled back on her reins, allowing the Silver Defendant to move to the front of her entourage. Racing upon a silver stallion, Stephen called, "Make way for the Princess of Kale!"

On the opposite side of the gate stood several men garbed in blue robes a few shades darker than would be found on the Defendant Team or within a temple. The guard of Serenitas was composed exclusively of former defendants: men and women who had served with honor before graciously deciding to step down and allow younger students admittance to the coveted team. One such man, Lord Yarin, a former Red Defendant, was currently serving as the captain of Lord Riccard's guard and it was he who rode up from the opposite side of the gate to greet the princess.

Ameria had slowed her mount to a walk by the time she reached the gates. Yarin was a middle-aged man with dark brown eyes and streaks of gray running through his dark hair. He gave a nod to the princess. "Forgive me, Your Highness," he said in a tone of surprise. "We were not expecting you."

"I did not inform anyone of my travels," she responded. "For security reasons, I am sure you can understand."

"Of course, princess."

"Please escort me to your high lord."

Yarin nodded, moving his horse to create a path. "This way, Your Highness."

Stephen moved his horse to the left of Ameria's, retaking his position at her side while the Red Defendant, Nicholas, moved to her right. Together they rode up and down a series of sloping hills and valleys until they finally came upon the estate of the high lord. The keep was as ancient as the temples from which its rulers hailed. It was a vast fortress of black stone which would be nearly invisible once full darkness settled over the land. A long series of black steps led to the tall, silver doors of the entrance. As Ameria rode, a small group of men emerged from the doors to greet her.

In the center of the group was a man of medium height and build with light brown hair and matching eyes. He wore a pair of black slacks with a long-sleeved dark green shirt which laced up the front with a weave of thick, black thread. He bowed at the approach of the princess, bending at the waist while the guardsmen around him dropped into a more traditional Kalian bow.

Ameria pulled her silver stallion, Argento, to a stop a few paces before the steps. The defendants pulled forward to stand on either side of her. She turned her gaze to the man at the top of the steps, who rose from his bow without awaiting her permission to do so. He then offered a broad smile in her general direction. "Greetings, my lady," he addressed Ameria. "My name is Lord Karris. Allow me to welcome you to the estate of the High Lord of Serenitas.

She nodded towards Karris before dismounting from her horse and handing Argento's reins to a member of the guard who stepped up to assist her. She ascended the steps with Stephen and Nicholas following closely behind her. When she reached the top step, she turned her attention to Karris. "Thank you for the welcome, my lord."

Karris nodded. "We were not expecting you, my lady. May I ask what brings you to our lands?"

"I have come to speak with the high lord," she answered. "Please inform High Lord Riccard of our arrival." She turned and began walking towards the doors, but stopped when neither Karris nor the Serenitas guard moved to follow her. She turned around, moving her attention back to the lower lord. "Is there a problem?"

"My lady," Karris replied. "I would be honored to assist you." Ameria tilted her head in slight confusion as Karris continued. "As Lord Riccard's chief advisor, I am well apprised in all matters concerning the realm of Serenitas."

"I am sure you are," she replied. "But I am here to speak with the high lord."

"Forgive me, my lady. But the lord is not to be disturbed with anything except the most important of matters. All other business concerning the kingdom is left to me." He flashed another perfect smile. "Can I not be of assistance, my lady?"

It was Stephen who responded first. "How dare you presume to speak to a princess of the realm with such—"

"Stephen!" Ameria spoke sharply, interrupting the Silver Defendant. She then turned back to Karris, whose smile had at long last begun to falter. "Tell me, Lord Karris." Ameria flashed a smile of her own. "Who am I?" She gave Karris the full weight of her sapphire eyes.

"Forgive me, my lady. I…"

Ameria shook her head, silencing Karris with the movement. "The king calls me, lady." She drew a slow, deliberate breath. "The queen calls me lady. Lower lords, like you, Karris," she deliberately left off his title, "address me by another title. Now I will ask you again…who am I?"

He looked at her as though dumbfounded for several moments and then finally said, "You are Princess Ameria."

"And who is my companion?" She motioned towards Stephen with a wave of her left hand.

"The Silver Defendant."

"Very good," she spoke condescendingly. "Now do you truly believe that I, a Princess of Kale, rode unannounced to the gates of Serenitas with the Silver Defendant as my escort and my arrival does not reach the level of the upmost importance?" Ameria took a single step, staring down at the low-level lord with her cold blue eyes.

"If I were you, Karris, I would be careful who I insulted. My sister is not fond of lords who never trained in the Kalian temples. I am beginning to see why." She took another step, closing the distance between herself and Karris to a mere breath. "Now take me to the high lord."

Chapter XXI

———◆◆※◆◆———

Princess Ameria was led into a vast room that rivalled any the palace had to offer. The walls were of the same dark stone which composed the outside of the building. A large fireplace stood against the wall opposite the door, filled with bright blue flames. In front of the fire stood two large chairs covered in dark blue velvet with carved gold inlaid along its edges.

Between the two chairs, standing with his hand upon a golden cane, stood Ameria's grandfather, the High Lord of Serenitas. At the age of seventy, Lord Riccard was a distinguished man. Though his long robes hung a touch looser than they had in times past, Lord Riccard still stood tall, the golden mark of Kale upon his breast hardly visible against the gold fabric. His silver hair was shoulder-length, held back by a thin, golden clasp.

Ameria stepped farther into the dimly lit room, until the reflection of the fire's blue flames began to slide across her temple robes. Then she paused, kneeling down into a traditional Kalian bow before the former Golden Defendant. She remained frozen in her position for several minutes, patiently awaiting her grandfather's permission to rise. He finally voiced his consent in a deep, sharp tone that had frightened her as a child. She rose gracefully in a single, practiced movement and turned to face the man before her.

It had been nearly ten years since she had last stood before her grandfather and she found herself nervous as she lifted her gaze to meet the high lord's piercing blue eyes. "Lord Riccard," she addressed him formally. "I request an audience with you, my lord." Her voice sounded far less confident than she would have liked.

"A princess of the realm does not make requests of high lords," Riccard informed her sharply. "A true princess, especially one who seeks to be a queen, issues orders and is subsequently obeyed."

Ameria's heart beat faster as she found her gaze sliding to the blue flames waving in the vast fireplace. "Have a seat, Your Highness," Lord Riccard instructed, motioning to the elegant chair on his left.

She stepped forward and seated herself rigidly upon the blue chair. She drew a deep breath before turning back to face her grandfather. "My lord," she began. "You are looking well."

"I look old," her grandfather stated. "Cut the court pleasantries, Ameria. I have no use for such nonsense."

"Really," she spoke without thinking, "This surprises me. Your chief advisor seemed fond of them."

It was Riccard's turn to sharpen his gaze. "Are you sure you wish to trade barbs with me, princess? I have been trading political insults since before your mother was born."

Ameria paused, catching his cold gaze before lowering her eyes toward the floor. "No, my lord. Forgive me. I…"

"However," Riccard said. "In your assessment of Karris, you stand correct. He is a fool. A childhood friend of your uncle's, Lord Andrew, who clings to my son's power like the parasite that he is. Still, questioning a princess marks a new low, even for him." Riccard gave a slight nod. "You did well to put him in his place."

"I would be happy to keep him there. If you find him as much of a disgrace as I did."

To her surprise, her grandfather offered a slight smile. "I would love nothing more than to allow you to do so. However, such actions would greatly distress my son, which as you can imagine, would likely make his pathetic attempts to run my province even more so."

Ameria fought to control her expression. She had never heard anyone in the court speak unkindly of her Uncle Andrew. Though, she had also never heard anyone speak particularly favorably of him either. Andrew, elder brother to her mother, had once served as the golden student of Kale, but lost the rank in the middle of his tournament year when his partner challenged him for the golden status. He had later fought in the famous thirteenth tournament the same year as Master Leo and Jiro, where he once again failed to live up to expectations, losing to Annabelle in a qualifying round and placing only twelfth among the top contenders. He then, from what she could recall, served Leo as a mid-level defendant for a few years, while his sister went on to become a Silver Defendant and princess. He now oversaw much of the day to day running of Serenitas, acting as an assistant to his aging father.

Not positive of how to continue the conversation, she shifted several times in her chair before returning her gaze to his. "I was surprised that

Andrew was not there to greet my entourage himself. I am, after all, his niece."

"Yes," the high lord replied. "Yet another sign of my son's incompetence." He paused, considering the princess for several moments before continuing. "However, I assume you did not come all this way to talk about my son."

"No, my lord." Ameria shook her head. "I came to you speak with you on a different matter."

"What would you have of me, princess?"

Ameria stood from her chair and took several paces closer to the large fireplace. She allowed herself several moments of silence, watching the blue flames sway back and forth across the thin pieces of wood which slowly crumbled to ash in the searing heat. The heat rose, sliding through the room to warm her pale flesh through a thin layer of gold satin. Her eyes began to burn, so she closed them, listing to the crackle of the fire and the beat of her own heart, before finally turning back to face the man seated behind her.

She reached her hand to her left hip and withdrew her hidden blade from its silver sheath. The sword reflected the dim light of the fire, the mark of Kale glinting upon its ancient handle as she moved the blade sideways, exposing it fully to the view of the high lord seated before her. Lord Riccard was unable to hide the shock from his face, his lips parting as though against his will. "Where…" He cleared his throat and tried again. "Where did you get that sword?"

Holding the blade tightly by its elaborate hilt, she moved towards Lord Riccard, still seated in his dark blue chair. "Why, my lord? Have you seen it before?"

Riccard shook his head, never removing his eyes from the enchanted blade. "No one has seen that blade. Not since the time of Kale." He drew a long breath and repeated his question. "Ameria, where did you get…the sword of Kale?"

She met his eyes with her own piercing, sapphire gaze. "You know exactly from where this sword came." She made her words a firm, cold statement before taking a long step, her black heels shattering the silence between them. "Now, Grandfather…tell me, about the wraith."

Chapter XVII

◆⋅⋙⋅✴⋅⋘⋅◆

"STORIES OF THE WRAITH ARE as old as the tales of the Gods themselves." Lord Riccard began. "They are embedded deep into our myth, rising and falling with the turn of the centuries."

"But when?" Ameria demanded of her grandfather. "When do they arise? What causes them to return, after centuries of absence?"

"Not what," her grandfather corrected her. "That is not the right question."

"Then who?"

"The Gods," Riccard replied.

"But why are they sent? Why are they here?"

"The wraith," Riccard's voice was cold, his face covered in the shadows of the dark room which shifted with the heartbeat of the fire's blue flames, "is the messenger of the Gods. Their legends are scattered throughout history."

"I don't understand," she replied. "Why are they here? Have you ever seen them?"

Riccard eyed her carefully. "I have studied their myths all my life. A hobby of mine; or obsession, if you prefer. But no, granddaughter, I have never seen the wraith of the Gods. Nor has any other living soul, until now."

"Who was the last one to see them?" she inquired. "When was the last time they were mentioned in the myths?"

"That honor would lie with Kale himself. Or Koloso, if you prefer."

"I don't understand. Why are they here?"

Riccard drew a deep breath, his shoulders straightening against the back of his velvet chair. "The wraith appears when the power of the Gods begins to wane. When history fades to legend and legend to mere myth. It is at those moments when the wraith arises, to re-establish the power of the Gods. To bear the vengeance of the Gods themselves upon a world which dared to forsake them."

The room continued to flicker in shadow and flame as she considered the words of her grandfather. "So," she finally said, "when the late king broke the oath of Blood and Arms, an act by which he foreswore his oath to the Gods…"

"He violated everything!" Anger leaped into the high lord's voice. "King Darek kept none of the vows which every king has been required to keep to the Gods since the time of Kale himself! He married outside of temple law. He removed their sacred monuments from the palace grounds. He banished their very presence from his court while instilling lords into the kingdom who would not know the meaning of duty, sacrifice, or service if the fate of the kingdom depended upon it! And I assure you, my princess, it most certainly does!" He paused to draw breath. "If the wraith is here, Ameria, King Darek is certainly to blame."

"You knew." What Ameria meant as a question came out as a statement. "You knew the wraith was coming."

Riccard gave a slow nod, his firm eyes staring into Ameria's. "They saved you, didn't they? In the woods when you were attacked. The cause of the slaughter to which no other in the kingdom has been able to explain."

Ameria's heart began to pound in her ears as she stared at the man before her. She had not spoken to anyone of the wraith, save for her sister. Drawing a harsh breath, she looked directly into Riccard's eyes and spoke the truth. "Yes, Grandfather. The wraith saved my life."

The high lord gave a slow, single nod and then said, "They have come for the twins of Kale."

"Yes," she replied. "They keep repeating a…"

"Prophecy?" Riccard offered. "Fear to the fearless. Hope to the hopeless. Mercy to those who hate you. Death to those who love you. That is your destiny, Princess of Kale, Princess of Koloso, Heir to Both."

Ameria stared at him, unsure of how to respond, when her grandfather continued. "When the people dishonor the Gods, the wraith is sent to remind them of their vows, their duty, and their mortality."

"And how," she asked in a voice that was almost swallowed by the darkness surrounding them, "does the wraith remind them of such a duty?"

Riccard looked directly into her eyes as he replied. "With the vengeance of the Gods."

Chapter XXIII

Mary walked down the rich red carpets of the palace corridors towards the private chambers of her mother, Princess Annabelle. When she reached the tall, black door to the royal chambers, the two guardsmen standing before the door offered a low bow in their deep, crimson robes. "Your mother is expecting you, Your Highness," the elder of the two men stated before opening the door before his sovereign.

Mary walked into the room to find her mother seated upon a plush red sofa in a long-sleeved gown of black satin. She had to resist the urge to kneel before her mother, still not completely accustomed to her new status. It was Annabelle who rose from the sofa to bow before her daughter to which Mary replied, "Please, there is no need for formalities."

Annabelle straightened with a swish of satin and retook her place upon the red cushions, motioning for Mary to take a seat upon the sofa across from her. "To what do I owe the honor of this meeting, Mariana?"

"I want to know about Nathan," she addressed the issue in a straightforward manner.

Her mother cleared her throat. "I already told you that he was a banished defendant."

"Yes," Mary stated. "Who was the father of Kevin, Peter, and Ryan; the men responsible for the death of both my father and Master Leo."

"I believe so."

"I told you that I would be back for the rest of the story."

Annabelle inhaled sharply before replying. "Yes, I suppose you did."

"Who was he? Why was he banished?"

"That is a complicated tale."

"Then explain it," Mary replied. "Explain everything."

"Well, it all started when your uncle, King Darek, decided to take Katerine for his bride. You're grandfather, High Lord Riccard, threatened the realm with civil war and called a massive army to his side to march upon the lands of Agnus. A group of defendants, which included your father, Nathan, and myself were dispatched by Leo to speak with the high lord.

"We had had spent two nights at the camp and Eadmund was still attempting to convince your grandfather to abandon his plans for war. The high lord had not advanced his army, nor had he ordered its disbandment. The arguments between your father and grandfather grew in intensity, continuing until the day that the Golden Defendant arrived at the camp.

"I was called to Riccard's tent and was surprised to find Master Leo standing across from my father. I offered a bow in his direction before stating, 'I did not realize you were coming.'

"'Well it seems I had little choice,' Leo responded. 'As no compromise can seem to be reached.'

"I suppressed a sigh and then shifted my gaze between the two men. 'Father,' I finally said. 'Do you still honestly believe that any good will come of this?'

"'You should be queen!' Riccard repeated for the umpteenth time. 'Anything less is merely a consolation.'

"'Consolation,' Leo entered the conversation. 'Tell me, my lord. Is there a consolation, in the entirety of the kingdom, which might satisfy your rage?'

"Riccard eyed Leo with a look that I had spent years of my life attempting to avoid. 'You use the word "rage" as though I stand irrational and unjustified, Lord Leo. As though the breaking and blatant disregard of our most sacred traditions is not an act worthy to merit the rage of those who are sworn to defend them.'

"Leo shook his head. 'I am not here to justify the king's actions, or to stay your anger, Lord Riccard. I am here only in an attempt to save the lives of the numerous brave men and women who will surely die if these provinces fall into civil war. Please,' Leo pleaded, 'keep your anger, if you will, but I implore you to find a means of expressing it that does not involve tearing apart the very fabric of this kingdom.'

"Riccard drew a deep breath and turned his eyes from Leo's. He stared at the far corner of the dark tent as though deep in thought before finally shifting his gaze back to me. 'I presume you agree with Lord Leo?'

"The question caught me off guard and I drew a deep breath to gather my thoughts before offering an answer as carefully as I could. 'It is not my place,' I finally said, 'to disagree with the Golden Defendant. Nor is it yours to disobey his commands, or those of the high priest for whom he speaks.'

"My father's deep blue eyes narrowed as he considered my words. 'Invoking the name of the high priest,' he replied, 'is perhaps the strongest argument that anyone has yet to make, daughter.'

"I nodded. 'His is the voice of the Gods...or so my father has instructed me to believe. To be obeyed at all cost.'

"'Yes,' Riccard exclaimed, 'a sacred commandment which the king has refused to uphold.'

"'That may be,' Leo interrupted from his place on the left side of the tent. 'But now you are also refusing his command, Lord Riccard, by not disbanding this army.'

"Riccard snapped his head towards Leo. 'Do you know what it would do to my status if I disband this army without any form of restitution? I would be seen as weak! A man who failed to stand behind his most core convictions! Who failed to defend his most sacred beliefs? I am the most powerful high lord in the kingdom! I will not be...'

"'Father,' I cut in, before lowering my voice to a more restrictive tone. 'Lord Leo has not said that you would walk away from this empty handed.' I turned my gaze to the man in the golden robes. 'I believe you were speaking of a...consolation?'

"Tension spilled into the room as both Leo and I turned to face the high lord. 'Consolation.' Riccard spoke the word as though it tasted sour upon his lips. 'Former Golden Defendants and current high lords should not be forced to settle for—'

"'Yes,' Leo interrupted. 'But the question is, my lord, are you willing to do so despite this?' Leo drew a deep breath. 'Are you willing to accept a compromise for the good of the realm, which you have always served above all others, both as a high lord and defendant is sworn to do?'

"Riccard drew several breaths before offering a deep sigh. Then he turned to Leo. 'If my daughter cannot be queen, as is her rightful place, then I would see her made a princess.'

"Leo's frame visibly tensed, and his head titled ever so slightly to the left. 'What?'

"'A princess,' Riccard repeated. 'If she cannot marry the king, then I would see her matched to Prince Eadmund.'

"'My lord,' Leo replied. 'The prince is already betrothed to Lady Lilian.'

"'I am aware,' Riccard nodded, 'perfectly aware that he is engaged to the daughter of a low-ranking lord in a match which never should have been allowed and could easily be pushed aside at the behest of the high priest, whose voice you claim to represent.'

"I drew a breath to speak, but was silenced with a cold look from my father, who, moments later, turned his enraged eyes upon Leo. 'If you want this army disbanded,' Riccard addressed him as though I wasn't in the room, 'you wish to quell my anger and save this kingdom from civil war? Eadmund is my price.'"

"Wait," Mariana interrupted as Annabelle's voice began to fade from the large chamber. "My father was betrothed?"

"Yes." She spoke the single word in a flat, emotionless voice.

Mary shook her head, moving to the edge of the sofa. "Are you saying that my father broke a vow of betrothal?"

"No," her mother cut in. "He never broke his vow."

"Then what happened?" Mary demanded. "Who was she? Why have I never heard this before?" She eyed her mother uneasily.

Annabelle raised her hand to her face, curling her fingers and pressing them against her cheek as she lowered her gaze to the floor pensively. Then she slowly lifted her gaze to meet her daughter's. "Lady Lilian was a Green Defendant from the Temple of Desoto. Your father met her in the tournaments, where they faced each other many times over years of competition."

Mary was confused. "Why would my father have been matched to a student of Desoto?" She shook her head. "To one of low rank?"

"It was not an arranged match," Annabelle replied with an incredibly guarded voice. "The king, your grandfather, had little interest in his younger son and offered no protest when Eadmund declared his intentions towards Lady Lilian."

"So you are saying that he simply…chose her?"

Her mother gave a curt laugh. "Yes. Just think, your father could have been the first royal in the Kalian line to marry for love." She laughed again, a harsh, bitter sound that seemed a perfect reflection of the loveless years she had endured as the esteemed Princess of Kale.

Mary allowed the sound to completely fade from the room before she spoke. "I don't understand. How did my father escape his engagement? Did the high priest declare he would marry you instead?"

Annabelle drew a deep breath and continued her story. "In all the years I spent by your father's side, I have never seen him as angry as he was the night Master Leo informed him of Riccard's demand."

Chapter XXIV

24 Years Ago

Leo walked towards the entrance of the large, black tent which Eadmund and Nathan were sharing. Annabelle trailed a few paces behind. When they approached the tent which housed the Kalian prince, Annabelle cleared her throat. "I should probably go," she informed the Golden Defendant.

"No," Leo replied. "I think you should accompany me."

Annabelle paused, gazing uneasily at the golden lord. "I am afraid, my lord, that this conversation will be difficult enough without my presence."

Leo stopped and turned to face the woman standing behind him. "What do you make of your father's demand, my lady? After all, it is you and not your father, who would have to marry the prince."

She stared into Leo's emerald eyes, taken aback by the question. "I will do whatever is deemed to be in the best interest of the realm, my lord."

An unnatural silence fell between the two defendants as Leo considered her carefully constructed words. Then Leo shook his head. "I know what you are willing to do, Annabelle. But I am asking…is this what you want?"

She stared silently at the Golden Defendant. A cold smile crept to the corner of her full lips. "Tell me, if I said no, would you turn from the spot on which you now stand, walk back into the tent of the most powerful and dangerous lord in the land, and tell my father that his demands cannot be met? Or would you instead, narrow those deep, emerald eyes, address me by my full title, and say that my personal sacrifice will save a thousand lives?" She paused for several heartbeats, then took a step, closing the distance between them to a mere breath as her long dark hair blew in a cold wind beginning to rise through the valley.

For several minutes, she stood perfectly still, waiting for a reply that she knew would never come. Then she leaned forward, moving her lips to whisper in his left ear. "I didn't think so," she drew back enough to once again stare into his dark eyes. "Go speak with the prince, Leo. I shall fulfill whatever duty you command...my lord." She offered a slight bow then turned and walked away.

Leo found himself resisting the unexpected urge to go after her. He stood for several moments in front of the black tent undisturbed, most of the camp's soldiers having either turned in for the night, or standing guard around the camp's outer perimeter. Annabelle's words replayed over and over in his mind as he stared intently at the blue grass beneath his feet. He could not figure out what it was about her answer which disturbed him so deeply or, for that matter, what had possessed him to ask for her opinion in the first place.

The look in her pale blue eyes conveyed a fierceness Leo had found in few others. He found himself wondering what fire lay hidden beneath her ever-present shield of formality.

"Would you tell my father that his demands cannot be met?" her words seemed to taunt him. *"I shall fulfill whatever duty you command."*

Leo drew several long breaths, a deep sigh filling his soul. *Perhaps in another life*, he thought, shaking his head to help free himself from the image of her piercing blue eyes and long, dark hair blowing in the wind. He then turned back towards the tall, black tent that stood a few feet to his left and entered to speak with Prince Eadmund. He was relieved to find the torches near the center of the tent still burning brightly with Eadmund, Nathan and Lilian seated in stiff, black chairs on either side of its limited light. All three stood at the sight of Leo's golden robes.

"My lord," Nathan addressed him. "I did not know you were here."

"I thought you were going to the palace," Eadmund added.

Leo gazed at the defendants standing before him before focusing upon Lilian, who had dropped into a traditional Kalian bow, her black robes pooling around her as the ends of her long, brown hair touched the ground. "Lady Lilian," Leo greeted her, unable to hide the surprise in his voice. "I did not realize that you were here. I thought you were assisting with training at the Temple of Desoto?"

"We asked for additional defendants to join our riding party," Eadmund answered for her. "Lilian volunteered."

Leo looked to his longtime partner and then back to the girl kneeling on the floor, then motioned for her to rise. "Forgive the intrusion, my lady, but I must speak with these two lords on an important matter. Please consider yourself dismissed."

"Yes, my lord," Lilian replied before turning back to flash a quick smile to Eadmund. "See you later?"

Eadmund returned her smile with a nod.

Lilian then turned and exited the tent, leaving Leo alone with the other two high-ranking defendants. As her footsteps faded from the room, Eadmund addressed the Golden Defendant. "What is going on, Leo?"

"Were you able to speak with Lord Riccard?" Nathan added a question of his own.

"Please," Leo answered, shifting his gaze between the two men. "I think we should all take a seat."

"Okay," Eadmund replied. "Would you care for a drink?"

Leo nodded. "Yes, thank you."

Eadmund nodded and walked to small, wooden table on the far side of the tent where he withdrew a small pitcher of red wine. He poured the dark liquid into a small, silver goblet which he passed to Leo before turning towards the small fire and retaking his seat across from Nathan. Leo took the cool drink in his hand and seated himself in the small chair which Lilian had occupied only moments before.

"To answer your question, Nathan," Leo began, "I have spoken with Lord Riccard and believe that there is a compromise to be made. However, I fear that it involved a rather…" he searched for the word, "complicated solution."

"Oh, and what solution would that be?" Nathan asked.

At this, Leo paused, staring into the dark wine before taking a long, slow sip. He then placed his silver goblet on to the ground beside him.

"Leo?" Eadmund inquired as the golden lord finally straightened in his chair. "What is it?"

Leo raised his gaze. "I am not…" His voice trailed to a sigh. He repositioned himself in the chair, his shoulders slumping as he leaned closer to the fire, the heat of the blue flames warming his skin.

"My lord?" Nathan asked from his left. "What has happened?"

Leo drew a deep breath before levelling his gaze to stare directly into his partner's dark blue eyes. "Eadmund," he spoke in a firm, steady voice, "Lord Riccard has agreed to disband his army, and rescind his threats against both the Lord of Agnus and the king."

"That's wonderful!" Nathan said, then paused when Leo did not remove his gaze from Eadmund's. "In exchange for what?"

"High Lord Riccard," Leo finally stated, "had conditioned the withdrawal of his army upon a single requirement." He leaned even farther towards the edge of his seat. "That you, my prince," he addressed his partner with an unfamiliar formality, "agree to take his eldest daughter, Lady Annabelle of Koloso, as your princess and bride."

Silence fell over the room interrupted only by the soft crackle of the blue flames which danced in a large circle between the three men, shadows dancing along the walls of the tent like lost souls in the dark.

Then, Eadmund looked into the eyes of the Golden Defendant and said a single word. "No."

Chapter XXV

24 Years Ago

IT WAS NATHAN WHO BROKE the silence. "I don't understand. Eadmund is engaged to Lilian. How can Riccard demand that he marry Annabelle?" Nathan stared at the two men seated beside him on opposite sides of the fire. The blue flames continued to cast their shadows around the large tent.

"Eadmund…"

"No," the prince interrupted. "No."

Leo moved both hands in front of him in a pleading gesture. "Eadmund please listen…"

"You marry her," Eadmund stated in a cold voice. "You're the Golden Defendant, the prize of Kale and natural choice to be the next Lord of Serientis. You marry her, because I will not."

"If it would solve this, I would do so in a heartbeat," Leo answered him. "But he doesn't want the next lord of his kingdom; he wants to see his daughter a princess." Leo found himself struggling to meet the rage in his partner's eyes.

"I will not do it," Eadmund said again.

"Riccard is talking about civil war!" Leo was unable to keep the strain from his voice. "He is talking about wiping the people of Agnus from the face of this world and he has the means…the power, to carry out his threats."

"I am betrothed!" Eadmund replied in an enraged voice, standing from his chair with such force that it clattered to the ground behind him. "In this kingdom," he continued, standing tall in his silver robes, "in our temples, which we are sworn to both honor and protect, a promise of betrothal is considered one of our most sacred vows! How, Leo, can you of all people ask me to forsake them?"

Leo closed his eyes and drew a deep breath, attempting to calm the emotions raging inside him. He stood from the chair, steeling himself against the anger radiating through his best friend's eyes. "My prince." Leo struggled to keep the emotion from his voice. "I do not ask this of you lightly, nor would I ask if there were another..."

"Send Riccard to the tower!" Eadmund exclaimed. "Remove him from power. Appoint another in his place. You are the..."

"He has an army!" Leo replied. "Two thousand men poised to rise to his call. Do you think they gathered here because he is some figure head? Riccard is the most respected lord in the land and he has been wronged; gravely and terribly wronged. And every single man standing in this tent knows it."

"So I am to pay for my brother's crimes?" Eadmund was almost shouting, his fingers curled into fists by his side. "My brother breaks temple law and I am to pay the price? How can you even begin to think that is right?"

"I don't!" Leo answered. "I don't think anything about this is right. But unless you want to challenge your brother for the throne..." He paused, lowering his voice as he said, "Do you want to challenge him? You are the only royal that is recognized as legitimate by temple law. It would be within your power to do so."

Eadmund took a step back, a look of near horror crossing his face. "You want me to kill...my brother? For a throne I don't even want?"

"I did not say I wanted you to kill him," Leo corrected. "I am merely pointing out that it is your only other option."

"Wait," Nathan interrupted, drawing both men's attention upon him. "Forgive me, my lords," he spoke slowly, "but aren't you forgetting something rather important?" Neither man replied, so Nathan continued. "If Eadmund was to take the throne from his brother, then he, and not Darek, would be bound by the oath of Blood and Arms. Which would mean that it would be his duty to marry Annabelle, as it was previously his brother's."

"I am not going to marry her," Eadmund returned to the original argument. "You cannot make me do it."

"Eadmund," Leo tried again, "I know how you feel about Lilian, but..."

"We are defendants!" Eadmund argued. "We are the best fighters in the land we can face any warriors. We could—"

"Could what?" Leo interrupted. "How many defendants would you have die so that you can have your bride? Whose life would you be willing to sacrifice in this civil war which could be so easily prevented? Whose life, Eadmund?" He motioned to where Nathan was still seated. "Nathan, the man you consider closer than your own brother, despite his Kolosian background? What about Angelia's, his wife? Jiro, who has on several occasions, saved both of our lives?" Leo levelled his gaze to meet Eadmund's head on. "Mine?" Leo paused, allowing his words to fill the room before slipping into the darkness beyond.

Eadmund finally answered in a tight, emotionless voice. "You expect me to what? Forget—"

"Your engagement to Lilian was not a match arranged by the Temples." Leo spoke. "Therefore, it can be superseded by a decree from the high priest."

"You have already spoken to the high priest?" Eadmund's voice spit venom.

"No. But he will approve the arrangement, for the good of the realm."

"The good of the realm? To lock me into a loveless marriage? To force me to betray the woman I love; that is what you consider for the 'good of the realm'?"

"If it saves this kingdom from war," Leo replied in a cold voice, "yes."

The tension in the room continued to increase with a strained silence. Then Eadmund moved his hand to the hilt of his silver blade. "Do you honestly think that you can force me to marry her? I am the *Sutis* prince of the realm!"

"Yes!" Leo's voice rose with each word. "You, Prince Eadmund, are the prince of the realm and the Silver Defendant of Kale! You have sworn your life to the safety and protection of the kingdom." Leo drew a deep breath. "It is your duty to help prevent this war by any and all means deemed necessary!"

Leo moved, sidestepping the blue flames which still burned brightly between them. When he finally reached his longtime partner, Leo gave a small sigh, closing and then opening his eyes. "If there was another way, I swear to you, my friend, I would do it. But…there is not."

"You cannot force me to marry her."

Leo gave Eadmund the full weight of his gaze, then slid his hand towards the golden hilt of his own Kalian blade. "Actually," he spoke in a slow, harsh voice, "you will find that I can."

It was at that moment when the first scream rose from the north side of the camp.

Chapter XXVI

24 Years Ago

Annabelle was seated in a small wooden chair staring into the slender flames of a small fire when she heard the first scream. She rose from the chair, turning to face the entrance of the tent. A middle-aged man dressed in the dark blue robes of Serenitas raced inside, causing her to instinctively draw her silver sword in a fluid, practiced motion. The man froze at the sight of the blade, dropping to his knees before her. "Forgive me, my lady," he spoke in haste. "We are under attack."

"By who?"

"The men wear the gray robes of Agnus."

"Agnus is attacking?" Her voice held a touch of disbelief. "With the Golden Defendant in the next tent?"

"I was sent to warn you immediately."

She nodded. "Go back to your post."

"Yes, my lady." The man rose and left the room as quickly as he had entered.

Annabelle adjusted the grip on her silver blade and exited the tent to a chorus of indistinguishable voices shouting for troops to rise from their slumber and prepare for battle. Men poured from the tents, rushing to form ranks towards the outer perimeter of camp. She moved to where she had left Leo, reaching the tent at the exact moment the three men emerged in their brightly colored robes.

"They are saying that it is Agnus." She directed her words to the Golden Defendant. "They are attacking from the northern side of the camp."

"Dammit!" Leo exclaimed. "What the hell are they thinking? Riccard's army is twice the size of Agnus'."

"Since when has that ever stopped the king?" Annabelle asked.

"The king?" Nathan inquired. "You don't actually think that the king order this attack?"

"Like the Lord of Agnus would attack my father without his blessing. Especially with the Golden Defendant in the camp!"

"What does it matter?" Leo interrupted. "The camp is under attack. We must form ranks."

"What can we do?" Additional voices joined the group as Annabelle turned to see Lady Lilian, garbed in her black defendant robes, had appeared alongside them along with Jiro and two lower ranking members of the team.

Annabelle turned back to Leo. "Will they stop if it was on our orders?" She shifted her gaze between the Gold and Silver Defendants.

"I doubt it," Leo replied. "However we have to at least say that we tried." His eyes searched the gathered party. "Angelia, Andrew," he addressed the two additional members of the team dressed respectably in robes of blue and white, "we need to—"

"My lord," Jiro, dressed in Red, called out as he rounded the corner to address the gathered group. "Additional forces have attacked from the west."

Leo drew a sharp breath. "Okay. We will split into two groups. Lilian, Nathan and Angelia will accompany me to the north side of the camp; Eadmund, Annabelle, Andrew, and Jiro to the west. See if they will stop when they realize actual defendants are leading the defense of this camp. If not, assist Riccard's men to the best of your ability." He moved forward, the gathered group parting before his golden robes. "Try to spare lives, if you can."

The horses had been tethered in a field near the center of the camp and servants had already rushed to prepare them for the defendants' arrival. They mounted their respective rides as indistinct cries began to rise through the camp. Orders were issued from afar and men raced towards the outer perimeter to join the fray.

"Where is my father?" Annabelle asked one of the men exiting a nearby tent with a sword in his hand.

"He rode out to lead the northern defense," came the answer.

Annabelle managed to maneuver her horse to ride as fast as she could through the scattered crowds. "Make way for the defendants!" She attempted to raise her voice above the crowd. "Make way for the defendants!"

The path was lit by dim torchlight, but it still took five minutes to reach the edge of the crowd and another two of hard riding to reach the outer edge of the vast camp. They heard clashing metal before the actual battle came into view. Annabelle pressed her heels into the side of her mount at the sound, urging her silver stallion to even greater speeds as she raced to join the battle. As the field came into view, a string of men garbed in dark blue robes stood facing off against a different group in gray. Men holding tall, blazing torches stood on both sides of the armies, the white flames lighting the field of battle so brightly that she had to resist the urge to close her eyes as they emerged from the surrounding darkness.

Blood had already begun to splatter the ground, perfuming the air with the smell of dying men, their cries masked by the sounds of battle. As they reached the edge of the battle, Annabelle slowed her horse enough to slide to the right side of Eadmund's golden steed while Jiro moved to the prince's left. Several heads turned at the sight of their shimmering robes.

Jiro's voice fought to rise above the crowd. "Stop in the name of the Golden Defendant!" All four riders pulled to a stop approximately a hundred and fifty feet from the closest of the fighting men. "In the name of the Golden Defendant, the Prince of the Realm, and the High Priest of the Temple of Ziazan, you are ordered to cease this fight at once! Any who disregard this order will be deemed traitors to the realm and the Kalian temples!"

Several of the men paused in their efforts, seeming momentarily unsure with the arrival of the high ranking defendants. Annabelle moved her horse a step closer, pulling upon the tightly held reins. "To defy us is the face the fury of the Kalian Gods!" she warned, her voice carrying across the field.

"Lay down your swords!" the prince added his own command. "Now!"

They sat upon the edge of the field for a moment, wondering if her command might be heeded after all. Then, one of the men in gray rushed towards them, using the pause in the fighting to pass Riccard's men. He let out a loud roar as he moved towards the defendants, sword raised high in his hand. Annabelle took a single moment to glance at the men beside her, and gave a nod. She then dismounted from her horse, her feet touching the ground a split second before she pulled her sword from the side of her saddle. She took several steps and then paused as the man continued to run towards her. Moving both hands to the handle of her broad, silver blade, she faced forward with a bored looked upon her face, which was hidden in the shadows of the night surrounding them.

When the man reached her, Annabelle calmly raised her naked blade. He did not slow at her movements, but instead increased his pace, moving both of his hands to the hilt of his blade. She stared calmly and raised her own sword to meet his. The sharp silver sang through the air as she brought her sword up in a sweeping arc, her blade clashing against that of her opponent's with the powerful sound of ringing metal. The man's arm shot up, driven back by the power of the blow, throwing him slightly off balance. She used the momentum to her advantage, twisting her body into a tight spiral before turning to slide the sharp edge of her blade across her attacker's throat. With the blade having sliced through his vocal cords, the man could not even offer a scream as she stepped swiftly to the side, avoiding the nameless man's body as he fell to the ground, with a loud thud and a faint gurgling sound as he drown in his own blood.

Facing the crowd before her, Annabelle calmly leaned down and wiped her blood-stained blade into the blue grass before sliding it back into the golden sheath at her side. She then returned to her silver mount in a single stride. The entire incident had taken less than sixty seconds and, once again astride her horse, she turned toward Eadmund with calm eyes, awaiting his next command. They eyed the crowd in front of them for several seconds, then a roar rose throughout the crowd, more men in gray attempted to move, but this time were blocked by Riccard's men who stepped to meet them. As quickly as it had paused, the clang of metal resumed to ring throughout the field.

Annabelle turned to her longtime partner, Jiro, and exchanged a look before both turned to take their cue from the Silver Defendant. Eadmund stared at the rising field before he reached down and drew his sword from the side of his saddle. Jiro and Andrew followed suit and the four riders moved their mounts toward the surging crowd.

Chapter XXVII

―◆―❖―◆―

Princess Ameria decided to spend the night in her grandfather's ancient keep. "We shall speak more tomorrow," her grandfather has assured her as she rose to leave the room. "You may have your mother's old chambers in the east wing. Your escorts may stay in the southern halls. The defendants of Kale are always welcome here."

"Thank you," Ameria replied. "However, I believe that Lord Stephen may insist upon standing guard throughout the night."

The high lord nodded in consent. "Of course, princess. The Silver Defendant is welcome to stay in the east wing as well; if it is your wish."

"I believe it will make him feel safer, to be allowed to do so."

Riccard nodded as he stood from his chair. "Allow me to escort you." With one hand on the top of his golden cane, Riccard offered the other to his granddaughter, who accepted graciously, sliding her right arm through his left. They moved towards the tall doors together, which were opened by a pair of men garbed in dark blue robes. The hallway was filled with freshly lit candles hanging from chandeliers lining the high ceiling of the ancient keep. Awaiting them, standing a few paces from the door, was Lord Stephen conversing with a middle-aged man with short brown hair and sharp green eyes. He was dressed in dark blue robes. As Ameria walked farther down the hall on her grandfather's arm, she made out the golden mark of Kale upon the man's blue robe.

The men's voices quieted at the sight of the pair walking towards them. Stephen dropped into a Kalian bow and, a few moments later, the man beside him followed suit. The high lord and princess continued to walk in silence until they reached the kneeling men. Riccard did not speak, but instead deferred to his granddaughter.

"Arise, Lord Stephen," Ameria stated as he rose in a swirl of silver. Then she switched her gaze down upon the other man. "I was surprised that you did not find it important enough to greet me when I arrived at your door, Lord Andrew."

Andrew raised his gaze, a look of surprise flashing through his eyes from his kneeling position. "Forgive me, my lady. I was in the middle of a very important—"

"It must have been important indeed," she replied in a cold voice, "to have been more important than the arrival of a princess of the realm; particularly one with the Silver Defendant by her side."

The older man stared up at her as though unsure of how to respond. "Forgive me," he tried again, "I meant no disrespect."

"Yet disrespectful," Ameria interrupted, "is what you were, Lord Andrew. I would be careful, not to be so again." She did not give him permission to rise, but instead glided past on the arm of the high lord. They walked in a slow silence until they reached the edge of the east wing, the Silver Defendant trailing closely behind them. When they arrived at the door, Lord Riccard nodded and released Ameria's arm. "Your room has been prepared, my lady. It is the third door on the left."

Ameria returned the slight bow and again thanked the older man before turning to walk down the hall. Lord Stephen moved to walk in front of her, stepping into the aforementioned chamber. She followed him a moment later. The walls were painted gold. A large four-post bed stood in the center of the room draped with golden curtains that opened to reveal a large, matching bedspread which bore the mark of Koloso in shimmering, silver thread. Somewhat surprised, she walked to the edge of the curtains cascading over the bed.

"This was once your mother's room," Stephen reminded her.

"Yes," she replied continuing to walk around the room. A tall dresser of dark wood stood on the left side of the wall under a large, silver mirror. Atop the dresser sat a series of matching golden trophies. Ameria stepped closer and picked up the center one. Upon the trophy lay the inscription: *Tournament of Kale Royal Championship: Lady Annabelle Berhea & Lord Jiro Darian of Koloso*. She traced her finger over the inscription, which was surprisingly free of dust. There were ten trophies sitting upon the desk overall, her mother having lost two of the twelve rounds in which she had competed; one to her own brother, Lord Andrew; her uncle's first and only victory over his younger sister. "She was very good, wasn't she?"

"Yes, my lady. They both were. Some even wondered if they might have surprised the realm and beaten the champions of Kale. But, well…we know that story all too well."

She placed the trophy back from whence it came. "Well," she spoke softly. "No use reminiscing, is there?"

"No, princess. I suppose there is not."

Ameria turned back towards Stephen. "My grandfather stated that you may use the room beside mine. I expect you to come quickly if I call."

"Yes, princess," Stephen stated before turning towards the door.

"Oh, and Lord Stephen," Ameria called. "I would advise not disappointing me."

Stephen did not reply, but instead walked silently across the carpeted room and disappeared into the hallway beyond.

Chapter XXVIII

24 Years Ago

At the sound of surrender, Jiro turned to survey the damage. Countless bodies littered the ground. Blood was running down his arms, mixing with that of those slain and saturating his formerly clean robes. The cut on his arm was deep, but not life-threatening. He also had a cut running down his left leg, but it was shallower than the one on his arm. It would likely require only a thin bandage until he could return to the healing chambers of the temples. His eyes searched the field before finally landing on Leo, who appeared uninjured as he walked closer to the camp with Lord Riccard by his side. Jiro walked briskly towards the other two men, doing his best to avoid stepping on the dead men at his feet. He raised his arm in slight greeting and then addressed the higher ranking lords. "What should be done with the wounded?"

It was Riccard who answered. "If the injuries are not life-threatening, then offer assistance. Otherwise…" He turned toward Leo, though whether in challenge or seeking permission, Jiro was unsure. "Otherwise…make it quick."

When Leo did not respond, Jiro gave a nod of consent. "I shall issue the orders, my lord." Jiro then turned and walked several paces to the left, repeating the orders of the high lord to the surviving soldiers who had begun to gather. Then he turned and walked through the vast graveyard. He avoided those who appeared the least injured, leaving them to be treated by those of softer hearts.

He walked until he came across a middle-aged man sporting a large gash across his stomach, his intestines exposed. He was one of Lord Riccard's, dressed in the dark royal blue of the Serenitas' Guard. Jiro looked down upon this man with a sad sense of resignation. "Help me, my lord," the man spoke in a gurgled voice, blood trailing down the corner of his mouth. "Please."

The Red Defendant met the man's brown eyes and forced a sorrowful smile. "You fought bravely," he told the dying man. "You have earned your place in the silver halls of the Kalian Gods." Jiro moved his hand to his side and, without warning, slid his blade deep into the man's chest, driving his sword through the heart with expert precision. A gasp was all that escaped his lips before his eyes glazed over and the spark of life he had clung to so desperately vanished. Jiro then withdrew his soiled blade and continued to walk through the field of bodies.

Jiro would never know how long he stood in that field as he sent his fellow warriors into the realm beyond. He concentrated only on the task at hand, locking a part of himself away in order to carry out the orders of the High Lord of Serenitas. He had lost count of the number of men he had killed long before a voice interrupted his task. "My lord."

Jiro looked up to see a young man dressed in dark blue robes standing in front of him. "Yes, what is it?" Jiro inquired.

"Please come with me. It's important." Jiro turned and followed the unknown man towards the far side of the field. A few paces before the red grass beneath them faded to blue, the man stopped and turned to again face the Red Defendant. "Forgive me. I know that Lord Riccard gave orders about those gravely injured, but…" He pointed down to where a woman lay. Jiro stepped to where the younger man motioned. The woman's brown hair was matted against her skull. Blood streaked both sides of her face and a deep cut ran across her left cheek. Her right arm lay twisted at an unnatural angle and splinters of bone protruded from just above her elbow. The left side of her chest was covered with blood, transforming her green robes to a brown of dirt and blood. Her throat moved, indicating the woman was clinging to life, in spite of the blood staining the ground beneath her. It took several moments before Jiro's mind came to terms with the identity of the woman lying at his feet.

"Lilian." Jiro knelt beside his fallen teammate. He placed his hand on her forehead. Her skin was cold to the touch. Her brown eyes opened at his touch. She tried to speak his name, but her voice arose hoarse, barely even a whisper. Jiro grasped her uninjured hand while turning back to the man kneeling beside him. "Go find the Gold or Silver Defendant," he instructed. "Whoever you see first. Go!"

He then switched his attention back to Lilian's trembling form. "Hold on," he spoke as gently as he could. Jiro ran his hands over Lilian's body to check the extent of her injuries, carefully avoiding her mangled arm. The cuts on her face, though deep, had thankfully missed the vicinity of her eyes. However, the wound on her chest concerned him. Jiro ripped open Lilian's green robes, exposing the large hole in the left side of her chest, which had been pierced by a blade. Her ribs had been split open and her breathing came in shallow gasps, a consequence of the damage which had been inflicted to her left lung. Blood poured forth from the injury, layering the already blood stained grass beneath her.

Jiro pulled off his own shirt, flipping it inside out before proceeding to rip the material into several long strips. He glanced up and called to another man who was walking nearby in the same dark blue robes which marked the Serenitas Guard. When the man reached him, Jiro motioned for him to move to the opposite side of Lilian's broken form.

"Help me lift her," Jiro commanded. "We have to tie this around her side, or else she will bleed to death." The man nodded and knelt down as Jiro switched his attention to Lilian. "Okay, my lady," he spoke softly. "This is going to hurt, but it must be done." He turned his gaze back to the other man. "On three. One, two...three."

Lilian's body was lifted between the arms of the two men, and Jiro maneuvered the long strips he had torn from his shirt beneath Lilian's body, tying it securing around her, applying pressure to her left side. She was then lowered back into the tall grass, causing a sharp scream to escape her lips as her broken arm touched the ground. Jiro then grabbed another piece of the torn cloth and pressed it against her oozing wound, drawing another cry of pain from Lilian's lips. "Hold on, my lady," he said again.

"What is going on?" Leo's voice interrupted Jiro's concentration.

"Lilian has been injured," Jiro replied, glancing up to find Leo standing alongside Nathan. "We need to tie her arm as well." Nathan moved and ripped the sleeve of his red robes, tearing it into strips as Jiro had previously done with his shirt. He moved toward her crushed arm. Jiro moved one hand to Lilian's shoulder, holding her down as Nathan wrapped the make-shift bandage around her arm and cinched it as tightly as he could manage. Jiro found himself hoping that she might faint from the pain, but his hopes came to no avail.

Jiro looked to Leo. "We should send someone to find Eadmund," he informed his golden-clad superior. "Short of the temple healing, there is little we can do for her."

"Will she survive to the temples?" Nathan inquired.

"I don't know," Jiro answered honestly before turning to Nathan again. "We must find the prince."

"No," Leo stated.

"What?"

"The prince is on the opposite side of the camp. If we are going to have a chance of saving her, she must leave for the temple now."

Jiro glanced up, unable to hide his surprised expression. "But Leo, if she doesn't…"

"There is no time."

Jiro stared at him for a moment as though in consideration, then said, "I will saddle a horse and leave immediately."

"No," Leo stated. "Nathan shall take her."

Jiro was again surprised by Leo's words. "My lord, Nathan outranks me. Surely it would be better to have him by your side."

"Yes," Leo stated. "He does outrank you. I do not like having the top three defendants in the same place, as you well know. If there had been more warning, I would have ordered Nathan far from this battle, to ensure that the leadership of the team would remain intact, no matter what the outcome of the battle. Nathan is third in command. Therefore, he shall be the one to take Lilian to the temple. You, shall remain here and continue assisting with the injured."

"As you wish, my lord," Jiro answered.

It took several minutes to find and saddle a horse. Lilian moaned in pain as she was maneuvered onto the horse in front of Nathan, the fresh rags pressed against her slowly changing to red as blood continued to seep from her left side. As they were about to flee to the temple, Leo leaned forward and spoke to Nathan. "Remember," he whispered, "this woman is engaged to the Crown Prince of the realm. The fate of the very kingdom may very well rest in your hands. Ride swift and true. May the temple Gods see your quest is fulfilled."

Jiro stood silently as he watched Nathan ride to the far side of the field before disappearing beyond the horizon.

Chapter XXIX

24 Years Ago

Several hours passed before Jiro again saw any of the other defendants. He was called back to the center of the camp to hear the official casualty reports. From the information gathered, Serenitas had lost nearly a third of their forces, however even these tragic numbers seemed insignificant compared to the staggering losses sustained by the Province of Agnus. Well over half of their soldiers littered the grounds surrounding the camp. Men from both sides had gathered to move the bodies of their fallen comrades to be burned in mass funeral pyres while a select few were separated as arrangements were made for them to be taken back to the various lands from which they hailed. This was a special honor afforded to only those men and women whose lineage could be traced back to one of the thirteen Kalian temples.

Jiro entered Riccard's large tent to find the high lord once again facing off with the Golden Defendant while the prince stood silently by Leo's left side. "Riccard," Leo addressed him. "Surely you must now see that this war is not a viable option. Are we honestly going to endure more battles like this one, over the king's slight?" Leo paused, his eyes searching Riccard's features. "Is it worth the loss of even more life?"

"I did not initiate this attack," Riccard stated defensively. "And I have never backed down from a fight."

"My lord," Leo tried again. "Are you saying you want more of this? That you would throw away the lives of all your loyal, trusted men for the slight possibility that your daughter may one day become queen?"

"The king has broken Temple law!" Riccard's voice filled the tent. "Law passed down by the very Gods you have sworn to both honor and obey. Laws which I, and those who serve me, will gladly lay down our lives to protect. You think that we won this battle through either superior numbers or your," he made the next word sound like something foul, "superior, leadership? If that is what you think, then you are even more arrogant that I originally believed." He drew a deep breath. "No, Leo, we won this fight because the Gods are on our side! And if we are forced to proceed, then we shall prevail in the next battle as well. The Rite of Blood and Arms must be honored, lest the Gods themselves visit upon us a fate far worse than any which could be derived by the realm of man."

Annabelle, who had entered the room near the beginning of her father's speech, joined the conversation. "My lord," she spoke cautiously. "I have spent the last six hours putting hundreds of men out of their misery. Good men, Father; some of whom I even called friend. I walked up to each of these men, begging for my help, and instead of saving them, I was forced to take my blade and plunge it deep into their chests until their heart stopped beating. Please, Father, I beg of you as a defendant and as a daughter: let the king have his bride."

Riccard looked from Annabelle back to Leo. "If you wish to avoid further bloodshed, then my price remains the same as it did before the battle." He shifted his gaze back to Leo, as though speaking to him alone. "I want my daughter made a princess. My grandchildren heirs to the throne. It is the only act which will distil my anger and, appease the Gods above." He paused to allow his words to settle over those gathered. "The prince's hand to my daughter's. That is my price, Golden Defendant." Riccard then stood and moved towards the door of the large tent. "I will leave you to discuss these terms amongst yourselves. However, I would advise not taking too long as, after all, I do have a war to plan."

The tent fell to an unnatural silence as Riccard's advisors turned to follow him, leaving the four defendants alone in the command tent. Jiro exchanged a concerned glance with Annabelle, neither quite sure where this conversation would begin...or end.

After several minutes, Prince Eadmund finally broke the silence. "Leo," he addressed the higher ranking defendant. "Please, don't ask me to do something I cannot."

"Eadmund," Leo answered.

"No," the prince interceded. "I love her." He took a step and raised his right hand in a pleading gesture. "Please, Leo. I...I love her." The fight was gone from his voice, as though it had been washed away in the same river of blood which now stained the field surrounding them.

Jiro watched Leo draw a deep breath before he began to answer his longtime partner. "Eadmund," he began. "I'm so sorry, my friend. I would never willingly do anything to hurt you. Nor to take away your happiness; you know this. But, Eadmund, you saw the massacre that just took place." He took a step closer to the other man. "Tell me, my friend, my prince—

how do I justify an entire war, the lives of countless men and women, for the happiness of a single man? Even if that man is one I consider to be my own brother?"

"No, I am betrothed to Lilian," Eadmund returned to his original argument. "I can't break my promise to her." Then with more conviction: "I will not."

"I'm sorry, Eadmund. But you will not be able to marry the Lady Lilian." There was something in his voice that Jiro could not quite place.

"You cannot simply dictate my life, Leo. I refuse to allow…"

"Eadmund," Leo interrupted. "I'm so sorry, Eadmund. So, very sorry."

"I can't," Eadmund protested yet again, a hint of desperation entering his voice. "I'm engaged to Lilian. I promised."

"My prince," Leo's voice remained at a low, calm volume. "You were engaged and you may always love her, but…she will never be your bride." Leo drew a deep breath and continued to stare into his partner's dark eyes. "Eadmund," he said again. "I am so sorry."

"Why do you keep saying that?" Eadmund demanded. His eyes surveyed the room. "Where is she? And where is Nathan?" He began to walk towards the long strip of cloth which served as a make-shift door to the large tent. "I'm going to find her."

He had almost reached the door, when Jiro stepped in front of him, preventing the prince from leaving the room. "Move," Eadmund demanded, but Jiro refused to budge.

"Leo," Jiro spoke to the Golden Defendant without moving from his place. "You haven't told him yet?"

"Told me what?" Eadmund asked, turning back to where Leo still stood. "What is going on? Where are they?" Leo did not answer, causing the prince to take several steps and again ask. "Where are Nathan and Lilian?"

Leo continued to stare at the prince and again said, "I am so sorry."

A chill seeped over the room as the beginning of realization dawned. "Why?" Eadmund demanded, as though the question held the power to change the forthcoming answer. "Why do you keep saying that?"

"I am so sorry, my prince."

"Stop saying that!"

"Eadmund," Leo finally stated. "I regret to inform you that the Lady Lilian was gravely injured during the battle. Nathan escorted her to the temple healing chambers." Leo drew a sharp breath. "She did not survive the journey. I am so sorry."

Leo placed both his hands upon Eadmund's shoulders and repeated his words. "I am so sorry."

Eadmund's body sagged as he lost the power to remain upright. Leo caught him, guiding him to a chair which was fortunately only a few paces away. Leo knelt beside the chair, allowing Eadmund's hands to clutch tightly against his arms. Silence filled the room as all eyes trailed to where the prince sat, clinging to Leo, his body rocking back and forth in the chair.

"I am so sorry." Leo stated one last time. Then, Eadmund raised his gaze meeting Leo's emerald eyes.

"Get out," the prince stated in a deep, raspy voice.

"Eadmund, I don't think…"

"Get out," he said again, his voice growing in volume with each word. "Get out. Get out. Get out!" He stood from the chair, pulling Leo to his feet before pushing him forcibly across the room. "Get out!"

Leo turned toward the exit, motioning for the other two defendants to follow behind him. As they emerged, Jiro found himself squinting in the brilliance of the Kalian sunlight. He took several steps away from the tent before turning to face the other two defendants.

It was Annabelle who spoke first. "You knew the whole time?" she asked Jiro in an accusatory tone.

"I knew she was injured," Jiro answered. "I had no idea that she had died." He turned his attention to Leo. "How do you know she is dead?"

"A messenger, but it doesn't matter…"

"The hell it doesn't!" Jiro challenged. "She has been gone for six hours. Six hours, Leo! And the prince didn't even know she was injured? What the hell were you thinking? I knew we should have let him see her before we," a wave of nausea washed over him. "We didn't let him say goodbye."

"Jiro!" Leo cut through his rant. "We did what we had to and it was my call to make. Mine, not yours!" His voice was sharp, lacking even the slightest hint of the sorrow he had expressed only moments before. "Now, there is nothing you or I or even the prince can do about what has happened here today. But what I can, and will do, is ensure that no further loss of life comes to this quickly dividing kingdom."

Jiro took several breaths to collect himself and then asked in as neutral a tone as possible, "What would you have of me, my lord?"

"You will remain here. Stay by the prince's side, at all costs." He then turned to Annabelle. "You, my lady, are coming with me."

"Where?" she asked softly.

Leo gave her the full weight of his gaze. "To make you the next Princess of Kale."

Chapter XXX

24 Years Ago

Leo's presence was announced by a member of Riccard's personal guard as he entered the small black tent where the high lord stood conversing with several lords of lower rank. "My lord," the guard manning the door to the tent announced. "The Golden Defendant and the Lady Annabelle."

Riccard looked up from the papers which covered the make-shift table in the center of the tent. "Well," the former Golden Defendant addressed the current. "Do we have an answer?"

"In private, please," Leo requested. Riccard nodded, waving to those gathered who turned and filed from the room. A few moments later, the two defendants found themselves alone with the high lord.

Riccard eyed his daughter for several moments before turning to Leo. "So," he spoke firmly, "have you come to tell me we are having a war after all?" He gave a hard look. "You know, I could always extend the offer I made to the prince to you. Join me. Defeat the king and, once we achieve victory, I will place you upon the throne."

"Me?" Leo responded with a harsh laugh. "And why would you put me on the throne, Lord Riccard, once it is yours for the taking?"

"I am not a natural heir - you are. As the great-grandson of King Fredrick III, your claim upon the throne would be legitimate in the eyes of the Gods—as would that of your child, which would be begotten from my daughter, of course."

Annabelle was unable to suppress the anger that began to slide over her features, listening to her father plot against now not only the king, but the prince as well. Her feelings must have been plainly visible.

"Oh, don't be so dramatic, Annabelle," her father addressed her. "The throne requires Blood and Arms. Leo is second in line to the throne. If

Prince Eadmund cannot be brought to reason, then Leo would satisfy the requirement, thus staying the anger of the Gods."

"That," Leo stated, "will not be necessary."

"Oh? Has the prince finally come to see reason?"

Leo took a step closer to the older man and then, in as cold a voice as Annabelle had ever heard, Leo replied. "The impediment to the marriage of your daughter to the Crown Prince," he paused, though for consideration of his words or for simple effect, she was uncertain, "has been removed."

"Removed?"

"Yes, my lord. Call off your army. Your daughter will be the next Princess of Kale."

"And what assurance do I have, my Lord Defendant, that the prince will neither change his mind on this matter, nor return to his former affianced?"

"She died," Annabelle answered softly.

"Ah," Riccard replied. "I see. I suppose you are correct; that has likely solved the problem."

"Solved the problem?" Annabelle asked in disgust. "Removed the 'impediment?' You are talking about a fallen defendant! Someone you, Leo, called 'friend.' She was your partner's fiancé, for Gods' sakes!" She turned towards the Golden Defendant. "How can you be so…cold?"

Leo looked at her with blank eyes that sent an unexpected chill racing down Annabelle's spine. She realized with a start that there was a side to Leo that she had never seen before. She watched in silence as he ignored her questions and, instead, turned back to address the high lord. "In light of this information," Leo stated, "is it safe to assume that we can now agree to disband this army you have gathered, and to cancel or at minimum, forestall, any upcoming battle plans?"

Riccard gave a single nod. "Wedding arrangements will begin…"

"As soon as those for the funeral are completed."

"And Eadmund?"

"Will offer no objections. He knows what is expected of him. He is, after all, a Prince of Kale."

"Give me your word," Riccard replied, "and I shall withdraw my army within the hour."

"You have it," Leo answered without the slightest hint of hesitation. "You have my word as the Golden Defendant, the prince shall fulfill his duty. Your daughter will be a princess within a fortnight."

"Very good," Riccard replied. "Very good."

Chapter XXXI

"So," Mary interrupted her mother's story. "Lilian died and you became a Kalian princess."

Annabelle nodded. "You asked for the truth."

She studied her mother for several long moments. "Did you ever love my father?"

"Love is a complicated term, Mariana."

"Did you?"

"I had immense respect for your father. I could not have asked for a better companion in my role as a princess, nor a better prince for the realm. He would have made an excellent king and I mourn the loss of such a man." She drew a deep breath. "But if it is a romantic answer you seek, I am not sure it is one I can readily give."

Mary sat silently for several moments. "I wish he was here."

"As do I," her mother replied. "I know this transition has proven difficult for you. I know it is not the future you had been trained for and I am sorry for that. Yet, it is our reality nevertheless."

There was a deep ache inside of Mary's chest. "It's not just that. I...I never thought that I would fight in this tournament without him there to see it."

Annabelle nodded. "There is no need for me to tell you this, daughter. But he was very proud." She offered a tight smile. "You need not fear. He will see the fight. He will be watching you from the golden halls, with the Lords of Kale by his side."

Mary looked at her long absent mother with unexpected gratitude. "I know that you want Ameria to win this fight, but I hope..." She searched for the right words. "I hope that I bring honor to you as well, no matter what the outcome."

Annabelle stared at her daughter and placed her hand upon the younger woman's shoulder. "I am certain that you will, Mariana. I know that I am not warm. It was not something I was taught to be. But I do want you to know that I do feel pride at having you for a daughter. You have brought honor to your temple, your kingdom, and your royal title. No defendant—no mother -could ask for more than that."

Mary paused her, uncertain as to how to respond before finally stating, "Thank you, Mother. I hope I never give you reason to think otherwise."

"I am sure you will not," she replied, removing her hand from her daughter's shoulder.

A moment of silent passed then Mary said. "There is still something that I do not understand."

"What is that?"

"Father was engaged to Lilian and then she was injured in the battle and died. But I don't see what this has to do with Nathan. Why was he banished?"

It was Annabelle's turn to stare in silence, her pale eyes staring deeply into her daughter's sapphire gaze. "Are you sure you want to hear it, Mariana? You may not like it at the end of the story."

"I am supposed to be a ruler—"

"Mariana," her mother interrupted, a strain in her voice that Mary could not quite place. "Let me be clear. You will not like what I am about to tell you. In fact, great pains were taken by many people to ensure that you would not ever need to know of it."

"What are you talking about? They killed my father because of what happened to their own. I need to know what act required such vengeance."

Her mother waited for several moments and then nodded. "Lilian was gravely injured during the fighting. The odds of her survival were slim. Prince Eadmund rode from the battle grounds to the temple where Nathan had taken her body. Eadmund was inconsolable. He demanded to see the body, still dirty and broken from the injuries sustained. Jiro rode with the prince, a day ahead of Leo and myself. When I arrived, Jiro was on the outer steps of the temple awaiting me.

"'I need to speak with you,' Jiro stated.

'Can it wait until I have had time to refresh?'

'No. It can't.' Jiro pulled me into the Temple and down several hallways until we entered a side room where he stood by a heavy door.

"'What is going on?' I asked him.

"'Something is not right.'

"'What?'

"'Did you see a messenger approach with news of Lilian's death?' he asked me. 'A rider from the Temple or such?'

"'No,' I replied. 'But then, I was a little busy.'

"'I never saw anyone ride up and the timeframe, it was so close. I have trouble understanding how they could have reached the temple and had time to send a rider back to Leo. Even on a golden horse it would be difficult to have delivered the news so quickly.'

"'Okay,' I said, confused.

"'I've asked others. No one seems to know who told Leo or how, exactly, he found out that Lilian had died.'

"'What does it matter? I don't understand this line of questioning.'

"'I saw Lilian before she left. She was in bad shape and I was uncertain if she would survive. But, well…I went in to take food to the prince and saw the body. There was an injury in her upper chest, close to the neck. I…' He shook his head. 'I could be wrong. I mean, there was a lot of blood and I saw so many injuries that day. But…'

"'What is it?'

"'I don't remember that cut. Not one near the neck. You would think I would have remembered one so close to the throat. But I don't.'

"'You think she sustained additional injuries during the ride?' My eyes widened. 'Forgive me, Jiro, but am I understanding your implications correctly?'

"'When Nathan left the battlefield, Leo said something to him. He reminded him that Lilian was engaged to Eadmund and that he should remember that the fate of the realm rested on his ride. It seemed…I don't know.'

"I stiffened at the implication in his words. 'Jiro, what you are implying is dangerous. You can't honestly believe that Leo would…that he would.'

"'I don't know what I am saying.'"

"Wait," Mary interrupted her mother's story. "You are saying that Leo ordered Nathan to make sure that Lilian did not survive? You cannot be serious? I mean…I know you two were rivals but this." Mary stood from her seated position to momentarily tower above the older woman. "How dare you? Leo was a hero!"

"Mariana," Annabelle cut in. "Sit down and listen."

"Leo would never do that! Order the death of a fellow defendant? I don't believe it. I won't believe it."

"Mariana, listen to me. I am not saying that Leo gave the order. But…I am not saying that he did not, either."

"I don't understand."

Her mother drew a deep breath. "Nathan was questioned. He stated that there had been an additional attack while attempting to escape the battlefield, yet no evidence of such an attack could be found, save for the single wound upon Lilian's neck. The artery that was cut caused her to bleed out in minutes. There was no way she would have reached the temple alive. Eadmund went ballistic at hearing the news. Accusations were raised from all sides. Some believed Nathan's story. Others thought he had killed Lilian for the good of the realm—to avoid the further bloodshed that my father, your grandfather, threatened. And others, though not many, believed that Nathan acted upon Leo's express orders."

"And what did you believe?"

"I believed Nathan. He was a friend, a fellow Kolosian and a high-ranking defendant. I never believed that he could have killed her. But it was not for me to decide. Eadmund was furious when the rumor arose that her death might have been the result of foul play. He went to Leo in a rage. They drew down on each other, and with a blade in his hand, your father defeated Leo. Nearly killed him before others managed to intervene." Annabelle shook her head, reeling from the memory. "The valley was searched for any who may have seen what happened. In the end, your uncle, under pressure from your father, found Nathan guilty of killing Lilian and sentenced him to death. Leo intervened, using the power of the temples to commute the sentence to exile."

"Did he do it?" Mary asked. "Did he kill Lilian?"

Annabelle drew a deep breath. "I think the only person who knows the answer to that question...was Nathan."

"And Leo's involvement?"

"Leo was the Golden Defendant, the Champion of Kale, cousin to the king and beyond all possibility of formal inquiry...even by your father. Nathan was not so lucky. I don't know if he was involved, but I can say that if he was..." She turned to gaze directly into her daughter's eyes. "If he was involved, then a grave wrong was committed again Nathan. A wrong that, at long last, has been avenged."

Mary stood from the chair, all air of familiarity gone as she stared down at her mother not as a daughter, but the Royal Princess of Kale. "I don't believe it," she stated again. "Leo would never have ordered the death of a defendant. Never."

"Tell me this, Mariana." Annabelle stood, gathering herself to her full height as she stared at the acting queen. "I have answered your questions. Now answer mine." Mary stared at her mother and awaited her words. "You have no desire to sit upon the throne. None whatsoever. Let's not bother denying this fact."

Mary offered a slow, careful nod. "Yet as you pointed out, Your Highness. This is our reality."

"Tell me, daughter. Is it you who desires to be queen or is it instead the teaching, the drilling, and control which, even now, Master Leonardo holds over you? Is it really so inconceivable that he would do anything to protect the kingdom and the honor, the power, of the temple he devoted his life to?"

"Leo protected the defendants. He protected his people. He would never have done such a thing."

"Yes. He protected his people. How many of them would have died had a civil war arisen from the lust of one prince and the stubbornness of another?" Annabelle took a step closer to the younger woman. "And while you search for such answers, consider this. What is the happiness of one princess compared to honor and glory of ensuring the kingdom has a Kalian queen? I ask again, is your desire for the throne your own, or your master's?"

A thousand words flew through Mary's mind, her anger simmering, yet they refused to form upon her lips.

"Mariana, there is no shame or loss of honor if you were to choose a different path. Golden student of Kale, Golden Defendant, and Master of the Kalian Temples. That could be your legacy. One matched by only the master who trained you."

"And if it were Ameria?" she demanded. "Would you tell the same to the daughter of Koloso?"

"If she did not desire the throne, then yes. I would be proud to see Ameria as the Temple Master of Koloso. But, she does desire it, Mary. Your sister has followed politics of the court all her life. You did not."

"And whose fault is that?"

"You never expressed an interest."

"How would you know? You never came to see me, you never sent news or answered any letters. You were supposed to have been my mother for Gods sake!"

Annabelle drew a deep breath. "I cannot undo the past, Mariana. Nor can I change my nature. I can only offer my counsel now and assure you that publically, no matter what path you choose, I shall be there to advise and assist you in any way I can… Your Majesty." She offered a curtsy before her daughter, bowing her head.

Mary returned the motion somewhat less gracefully, then turned and left the room.

Chapter XXXII

------ ✦•◦✤◦•✦ ------

Princess Ameria walked the grounds of her grandfather's stone fortress. Built over a thousand years before, the ancient walls stood as a testament of the power of the family which resided within. The maternal side of Ameria's family was as ancient as that of her father's and almost as royal, tracing their lineage back to the time of Kale himself. The royal line was littered with the daughters and sons of Serenitas and closely related marriages were not uncommon among the royal family. In fact, Master Leo himself had been a relative of both bloodlines. Leo's grandfather, Lord Brunit, had married Lady Xandra, Lord Riccard's sister. Brunit had been the son of Prince Gregory who was the son of King Fredrick III, Ameria's own great-great grandfather. Leo's sister, Lady Jessa, had married the third son of the High Lord of Periculum. Their son, Marcus, had been Mariana's partner.

Kyle was also a descendent of royal lineage. His grandmother, Princess Dahlia, had been the youngest daughter of King Fredrick IV, making both Kyle and Marcus the great-great grandchildren of King Fredrick III. Ameria's own lineage could also be traced back to Fredrick III. Her father, Prince Eadmund, was the son of King Nicholas III, whose father was King Fredrick IV, the son of King Fredrick III. It had always been interesting, though not surprising, that she, Marcus and Kyle were all the great-great grandchildren of the same man, yet their families could not have been further apart. They were rivals in everything from temple loyalties to their traditions, to their very core beliefs in the Gods above.

She walked down a path that surrounded the castle of Serenitas. Stories said that Koloso himself had once walked along these ancient stones. She wondered if he had ever looked up with the same wonder that she now found herself, or with any inkling that his story would survive so far past his lifetime. Ameria finally reached the back of the grounds and walked up a set of stairs leading to the stone terrace. She walked to the edge, placing her hand upon the stone wall that reached her lower chest, gazing out over the land. Only two of the three suns were visible in the violet sky. Long strands of blue grass covered the ground between sparsely placed trees, the limbs swaying in the breath of a cool morning breeze. Her golden robes swirled lightly in the wind and she could not help but wonder how, in all the years of her life, her mother had never once brought her to see this beautiful land.

"Enchanting, isn't it?" She turned to find her grandfather standing only a few paces behind her. He took several steps, leaning upon the golden cane in his hand as he walked towards the edge of the stone terrace. "This is my favorite view of the grounds. I come up here every morning to watch the sun rise, and each evening to watch it set. In all my travels, in all the kingdom, there is no place I would rather be."

"I can't believe I have never been here," she found herself voicing her thoughts.

"You were, once," her grandfather spoke while continuing to stare out into the horizon. "You were four, perhaps five. You were on your way to the temples, and your mother brought you here. Do you not remember?" Ameria searched her memories, but could remember no such occurrence. "Well, you were young," her grandfather stated. "Perhaps it is for the best."

"What do you mean?"

Her grandfather continued to gaze forward, not looking at the princess standing beside him. "When you were born, there was a great celebration in this land. A child of Serenitas born at last with the title of princess. It had not happened in many generations. A daughter of two Kalian champions. It is no surprise to me that the throne now lies between you and your sister. I told them all those years ago that the Gods would not bless a temple-less queen with children, and the Gods have seen my warning fulfilled. When you were finally brought to my doors, I knew that I was right to force the marriage between your parents. No matter what the price had been. Especially, after…"

"After what?"

"I does not matter."

"Yes, it does." Ameria turned her eyes from the fields to look towards the high lord. "I came to your for truth, Grandfather. If there is more I should know, then please tell me."

Lord Riccard finally turned his eyes towards those of the young woman by his side. "You are not soft like your father. I feared you would be. I am glad to see that you are not."

"Soft has never been something I have been accused of, my lord."

"Nor have I," he answered. "If I had had my choice, you would have been here far more often. However, it was not a choice that was ever given to me."

"Why would you have had me here, my lord?"

"Because you are as much a daughter of this land, as you are of the royal line."

"I don't understand," she answered. "You are a high lord and my grandfather. Why would I not have been permitted to be here?"

His gaze turned back towards the sky. "I remember you being here. You more so than your sister. Mariana was scared by the dark towers and the ancient stones. But you, Ameria, were fearless. You stood out on this deck, right here, and I lifted you to see the province." A slight smile crawled across his lips. "I am not a sentimental man, Ameria. I am not a soft man either. But that memory of showing you, my royal granddaughter, this land which I love is one of the few to which I hold a great deal of value."

Surprised by his words, Ameria remained silent, allowing him to continue.

"My own children had been a disappointment, with the exception of your mother, of course."

"Your children?"

"Well, yes. Or rather, your uncle, as your have witnessed with your own eyes."

Again, the princess chose to remain silent.

"You were here for several nights. The high priest had come here to hold conference over where you and your sister were to be placed within the temples. The ground seemed neutral, as the house of Serenitas had champions from both the Kalian and Kolosian temples. Several temple masters and high ranking defendants had come to offer advice upon the matter. Your mother, as you can imagine, was most adamant that Mariana serve at the Temple of Koloso, as she held golden status where your father held only silver. The Temple Master of Kale and Koloso both argued for the two of you to attend their respective temples. The Gold and Silver Defendants also argued as well. It was quite the scene."

"And you, Grandfather. What did you advise?"

"That you should each be sent to separate temples, to ensure you both had an equal opportunity to wear the golden robes. It was what I did with your mother and uncle."

"So, it was you who decided where to send us?"

"No." Riccard shook his head. "I advised the opposite. I would have sent Mariana, as the eldest, to Koloso to wear the golden robes of your mother and you to Kale, to the silver of your father."

"Then who decided…"

"It was the last night you were here. The negotiations were going nowhere. No one seemed to want to relent and all were beginning to turn to the high priest in order to make a final decision on his own. That night, you and your sister were placed in adjoining rooms on the opposite side of the grounds from where you are staying now. All seemed quiet, but then…" His words trailed to silence and he turned away from her sapphire gaze.

"What happened? Please tell me."

Riccard gave a deep sigh. "A strange sound came from the room. They said it was the sound of something large falling to the ground followed by a series of screams. Guards poured from down the hall, surprised to find that those posted outside of the doors were nowhere to be seen. The men who arrived stated that they had attempted to open the door, but found it sealed shut and no matter how hard they tried, they could not get into the room." He drew a deep breath. "More screams were heard and then they suddenly stopped and everything faded to silence. The doors opened." He paused again.

"What happened?" the princess demanded.

"I was not personally there. However, I did see the aftermath."

"The aftermath?"

Riccard nodded as the morning wind continued to blow her golden robes around her. "There were several men inside the room with you. Only, they weren't men…not any longer." Riccard turned to meet his granddaughter's gaze and a chill crawled up her spine. "The bodies lay in pieces across the floor. Bones pulled from flesh, blood splattered the walls. It was a massacre."

The chill turned into a full-blown shiver. "Like the one in the woods."

"Yes," Riccard replied. "I arrived a few moments after they had opened the doors. I reached your room first. You were sitting on the floor in a thin nightgown in a puddle of blood. Beside you lay the blade of the sword of the Temple Master of Kevera."

Ameria gave a hard swallow, the world seeming to darken around her. "A temple master?"

"Yes," Riccard answered. "They had tried to kill you and your sister."

"And the massacre was…"

"No conclusions were ever drawn. But…"

"But you knew," she stated, her words stolen by the wind.

Riccard eyed her for a long moment. "The men who entered your sister's room came out with a strange tale. One that many said was a figment of their imaginations. Shapes in the shadow of their shock and horror over finding the young princess in a pool of blood. Tell me, Ameria. What did they see?"

"A wolf," she answered. "A large, black wolf."

"Yes."

"They had come to kill us."

The high lord nodded.

"And the wraith saved our lives. Even then."

"Yes. Even then. I believe they have protected you all your life."

"Why?"

"Because of the prophecy. The one they whisper in your ears, every time you close your eyes."

"But what does it mean?" she implored him. "Heir to Kale, Heir to Koloso. Mercy and Death. What does it mean?"

"That, princess, is a question you must come to answer for yourself."

She drew a deep breath. "What happened, after that?"

"It was decided that it was too dangerous to keep the two of you in the same location and you would, therefore, be sent to separate temples. Master Leonardo, who had no children of his own, declared that he would take your sister as the heir to his golden rank. The high priest consented. The next day the two of you were escorted to your respective temples and never returned to the land of Serenitas again."

Chapter XXXIII

Mary sat upon the uncomfortable throne where she had been confined for the majority of the afternoon. Lords and ladies had come from many corners of the kingdom to beg an audience with their acting queen. She was reaching the end of her patience, listening to a dispute between the boundaries of two lower provinces, when Chiro finally stepped in. "I'm sorry," he stated to the long line standing behind the woman speaking. "But the Crown Princess shall hear no more speakers today."

The room was cleared. Mary placed her hand to the side of her face and rubbed her left temple.

"Forgive my forwardness, Your Highness. But you appeared tired."

"It's fine," she replied. "Any longer and I might have lost it." She shook her head and wondered again how she, who had been trained only in the art of combat and obedience, had ended up on her uncle's contested throne. Her eyes closed as she continued to massage her temples.

Lord Chiro walked across the silver floor, stopping at the bottom of the marble steps. "Your Highness," Chiro spoke softly. "With your permission I would like to assign these cases to members of your Royal Council. Which would free your schedule for more…" He paused, searching for the right word.

"Yes," Mary stated. "I would be most grateful if you would do so. Provided you come to me with matters of higher importance, of course. Anything from a temple master or high lord."

"Of course, Your Highness. I would never dream of handling matters of such importance and would always bring such matters directly to you."

Mary rose from the throne and descended the marble steps. "I fear, my lord, that in my attempts to run the kingdom, I have been remiss in other duties."

Chiro nodded. "If I may suggest, my lady, the restoration of the palace training room is complete. At least enough for the purpose of training.

When is the last time you practiced? The Royal Championship tournament is coming soon.

"Yes," Mary replied. "I suppose it is."

"Should I send Kyle? Or would you prefer a different partner?"

Mary winced at the word 'partner,' her eyes trailing along the silver floor that had been wiped clean of all traces of the blood that would forever stain her memories. Noting her expression, Chiro instantly regretted his choice of words. "Perhaps you would prefer to train with a defendant? Even Lady Rebecca herself?"

"No." Mary shook herself from the memory. "I would prefer to work with Kyle. Though I would be appreciative of a master to oversee the training. Would you please send Jiro as well?"

"Of course. I shall do so at once."

Mary nodded and walked towards the outer door of the throne room, her heels echoing against the silver marble. Exiting the tall silver doors, she walked down the long corridor with two of the palace guardsmen falling into step behind her without being asked. The training section of the palace had fallen into a state of disrepair over the years, her uncle refusing to pay for its upkeep. One of her first acts had been to restore the facility to its former glory. The project had been completed while she had been away dealing with the Lord of Usbqu. As Mary entered the vast chamber, it was to find a different room than when she had left.

The room stood as an exact match to the temple training rooms. It hosted six large mats, each colored to match the rank of those permitted to fight within them. They were draped in large curtains that had been freshly hung before each of the colored mats. Closest to the entrance was a set of mats on opposite side of a long isle which ran down the center of the room. On the left the mats were purple and white while on the right, they were yellow and black denoting the lowest ranks found within the temples. In the center of the room were the mats of mid-rank, blue and green alongside pink and red. Finally, at the back were the sections reserved exclusively for those of the highest ranks.

Mary walked down the long, crimson aisle in the center of the room, but paused when she reached the last section of the room. Her eyes trailed first to the section reserved for defendants and temple masters, draped in curtains of spiraling rainbows, the colors intertwining in the same order as the rank of the temples. She studied the swirling pattern for several moments, wondering if she would ever be able to fight in the most coveted area of the temple. *Not as a queen*, a voice whispered through the confines of her mind. Her heart ached at the thought.

"My lady." Kyle's voice startled her from her thoughts. "Lord Chiro said that you wanted a sparring partner?"

"Yes," Mary replied. "If you don't mind?"

"I am at your service, princess."

Mary turned to fully face him. "I'm not sure I can raise my blade with you calling me 'princess.' It doesn't seem right."

Kyle nodded. "As you wish then, my lady. In this capacity, I shall refrain from using your higher titles."

The strange formality caused Mary to let out an inappropriate laugh. The kingdom was on the line, her master had been killed before her eyes, Marcus was dead and yet here she was standing in a room debating the proper use of titles with the man she…it was absurd.

"My lady?"

Mary laughed again before stepping past the silver lord. She moved to her left towards the final mat against the back wall. Draped in shimmering cloth of silver and gold, this section of the chamber was larger than the ones closer to the doors, reserved exclusively for those of Royal Championship rank. Parting the long curtains, Mary walked across the mat until the floor matched the golden robes wrapped around her slender frame. Behind her, Kyle removed his outer robes and stepped onto the silver half of the mat. He wore a long-sleeved silver shirt which hung loosely around his arms. His shoulder-length black hair was pulled back with a thin silver band.

The two champions stared at each other for a long moment before Kyle asked, "With blades or without?"

"With," she answered, pulling the golden sword from her side. "If you are up to it?"

He did not answer but instead withdrew his own silver sword. He raised the blade, moving both hands to its hilt. "Do not expect me to go easy on you, just because some might call you a queen."

The words caused Mary to crack her first smile in days, the weight of her sword comforting, grounding her back to a reality that was familiar and calming. Here upon the golden mats with her blade clutched in her hands, she felt a sense of calm she had not known since taking the throne. Here, staring across at Kyle, she finally felt in control. Her heartrate steadied and her breathing slowed. She slid her leg back, balancing her weight as she held the blade in front of her.

"Shall we dance?"

He smiled and it lit his entire face. A rare, genuine smile which she could not help but return. Then, without warning, Kyle's blade crashed down upon hers. She held her ground, gripping the golden hilt tightly as the side of her sword slid along the edge of Kyle's. Mary stepped back, tilting her blade as Kyle again moved forward. His sword sailed towards her left. She parried, the blades clashing together, shattering the silence of the large chamber. Both swords were raised high, the edges sliding one against the other.

Mary twisted away and jerked her arm down. He followed the movement, stopping her blade mere inches from his stomach. He pulled back and turned right, swiping towards Mary's side. She twisted. The blade flew harmlessly through the air. Her heartrate increased. His blade came down. Mary turned her blade sideways, sparks flying between them. Then she swung her sword left. He parried. She used the power of the clashing swords to turn in a full, tight circle. Her blade flew towards Kyle's side. He stopped her only a split second before the sharp edge would have sliced through his skin. She turned, bringing her sword down, and he followed her movement. She jerked up towards his chest and Kyle moved back.

"My lady," he said. "We are not near the temple's healing chambers. Perhaps…"

His words froze as her sword again moved towards his chest. He blocked her blade with his own, the sound of their steel echoing through the empty chamber. She twisted again, her sword moving towards his left faster than most eyes could follow. He again matched the movement. Her golden blade moved up and down, each stroke more furious than the one before.

"My lady, wait," he stated between each deafening clash. "Mary!" He moved his sword against hers, then slid and swept her leg with his own, causing her to tumble towards the golden mat. He followed her to the ground, knocking her blade from her grasp. He tossed it aside along with his own.

Mary lay upon the mat for several moments attempting to catch her breath before slowly rising to her feet. "What are you doing?" she demanded.

"We are not in the temples, my lady. There are no healing chambers here."

"Are you saying that you couldn't handle it?" Her emerald eyes bore into his.

"My lady."

"Don't!" She stepped closer to the man standing in front of her. "Please, Kyle. Don't call me that. I can't take it—not from you."

He moved his hand to the back of her neck. "I don't want to hurt you. I would never forgive myself if I did."

Mary's eyes trailed to the long scar cutting above and below his jeweled eye. She touched his face, her finger tracing lightly along the scar placed so recklessly by her blade.

"Mariana." He leaned forward and pulled her into a firm, passionate kiss. She responded, running her hand along his cheek as the kiss deepened. For a moment she lost herself, seeping into the feeling of his lips against her own. Then she pulled back, staring into his eyes as though waking from a dream.

"I'm sorry," she said. She stepped across the mat, kneeling to pick up her sword as she did so.

He followed her, grabbing her arm as she slid her sword back into its place upon her hip. "Mariana."

"Blood and Arms," she said miserably. "I…I can't."

"I hear your screams, Mary."

Her breath caught and became more ragged. She leaned forward in spite of herself and kissed him as though she could pour a part of her soul from her lips into his. She pulled back gasping for breath, her eyes wild with pained emotion. "I love you," she said before turning to flee the room as fast as she could.

He watched her go before turning to gather his own blade from the floor. A thousand thoughts jumbled through his mind as he walked to the door and found himself standing face to face with his father.

Dressed in silver with the mark of Koloso on his chest, the two men looked remarkably similar. "So," Chiro stated. "Do you want to explain?" Kyle did not answer, prompting the High Lord of Turbamentum to step closer to his son. "Kyle," he spoke slowly. "She is a blood princess of the realm with the blessing of the temples. The golden student of Kale and the daughter of two Kalian Royal Champions."

"I know what she is."

"Then start acting like it. She is everything we could ask for—as long as she keeps her vows."

"Father, look at her!" Kyle replied angrily. "She's a girl. A tired, scared girl who never asked for any of this!"

"She is a queen," his father corrected. "Your sovereign queen who you are sworn to protect—even from herself."

Kyle glared at his father, but remained silent.

Chiro sighed. "I do not begrudge your feelings. But you also must never forget who and what she is." He took a step closer. "She is sworn to fight for the crown and the winner is bound by Blood and Arms. You may not win that tournament. For that matter, she may not win either. Ameria may yet win the crown and then where would you be?"

"I could always refuse the marriage."

Chiro did not yell at this but merely continued to stare calmly at his son. "If you win the tournament, you will marry the future queen. I don't care if I have to drag you down the aisle in chains. I will see you made the next king."

"You expect me to…"

"I expect you to honor the family name and the temple you serve."

"I could just not fight," Kyle threatened.

"Then you will be with neither sister, including the one you seem to be falling for. And you will never rise to the rank of an upper level defendant, for which you have trained all your life. Stop making idle threats—they are beneath you."

A long moment of silence passed between them before Kyle finally said. "What would you have of me, Father?"

Chrio eyed his son carefully. "Remember who she is. Help her if you can, but remember her vows and your own." Then he said plainly, "If you bed that girl, she will never be queen."

Chapter XXXIV

"I watched you fight once," Lord Riccard told Ameria. "It was your final fight at the Temple of Kale. I had followed your success, but when the news arrived that you might win all twelve tournaments, I decided to see the final fight for myself. You brought great honor to Serenitas that day. The youngest ever to become an undefeated champion. Not even your sister could take that honor from you."

"I was unaware that you were in attendance, Grandfather."

"No. I did not announce my arrival nor my departure. I wished to avoid a confrontation with your father that day. It would have been inappropriate to have brought our arguments to your celebration."

Ameria nodded. "Yes, my father was never a particularly forgiving sort of man."

"No, that he was not. He resented me for the forced marriage. I had hoped that once he saw the level of greatness that the marriage of our bloodlines had produced, he would see reason. But it was not so."

"I do not believe that my father ever thought much of me one way or another," she stated with a hint of bitterness.

"No, I would imagine not. He was, after all, Kalian. To their temple, most are loyal to a fault."

"But not you?" Ameria inquired. "You attended the Temple of Kale, as did your father and brother. Yet, you decided to send your daughter to the Temple of Koloso. Surely you could have sent her to Kale as well?"

"I knew that my children's greatest opportunity to become high ranking defendants lay in their ability to wear golden robes. At the same temple, both could not do so. Therefore, it was only logical to send them to the separate temples."

"And it did not bother you that the highest ranking of your children attended a temple that you did not?"

"Kale versus Kolsoso. Dektra versus Desoto. How quickly temple masters seem to forget that they serve the same Gods. Petty rivalries over insults so old that no one can remember what started them." He shook his head. "The Temple Masters of Kale and Koloso were equally capable, and both of my children were given the opportunity to wear gold." He sighed. "Even if only one of them was capable of maintaining such a status."

"Andrew lost to his partner, correct?"

"Yes, my son. Even then, a disgrace to his lineage."

"Did he compete in the Tournament of Champions?"

"Yes, and did not even break to the qualifying rounds." He shook his head. "You mother lost to the undefeated champions of Kale. She competed with the very best and earned her place within the history books of the championship tournament. If your uncle had broken even partially, his honor may have been persevered. But to lose without even breaking to the finals? To less than worthy opponents…"

A moment of silence passed between them before Ameria asked. "Did you ever see my sister fight?"

Riccard nodded. "A year later at the Temple of Kale."

"So, you saw both our final tournaments then." An unspoken question lingered.

"If you would like for me to state which of you I believe would win, then I will have to say I can give you no answer. All I can say is that you were both magnificent. The very essences of what one would expect from the Gods' chosen."

She considered him for a moment, and then took a chance. "May I ask you something, Grandfather?"

"You may."

"If I lose the fight…"

"Then you will know that it was as the Gods decreed." He moved closer to her. "So many people mistake loosing with dishonor."

"Is it not the same?"

"Of course not. Your sister is an opponent that all dream of. To face one as worthy as she, an undefeated Champion of Kale. There is no disgrace in losing to a worthy opponent. Your father lost the thirteenth tournament. Did that make him dishonorable, or his men less loyal to his command? No! He fought valiantly and maintained his honor. He went beyond that fight to help lead and defend his people both as a high ranking defendant and as a prince of the realm. We had our differences, it is true, but no man could call your father less of a hero for wearing robes of silver instead of gold; not when the undefeated champion of Kale wore the golden. You and Mariana are equally matched. No one will look down upon you, should you lose to your sister. The loss of honor occurs only from losing to one less than worthy, as your uncle once did." He looked

129

directly into his granddaughter's eyes. "Fight with honor and believe in the Gods above, no matter what the outcome."

Ameria bowed her head. "I thank you for your wisdom, Grandfather."

Chapter XXXV

―⋅≍⋅✵⋅≭⋅―

Kyle stood before a large stone door. The shadowy hallways, lit dimly by torchlight, were silent. Finding nothing but darkness on either side, he turned back to the door and reached for the black, iron handle. He pushed lightly and the door opened with a loud creak. He stepped carefully over the threshold.

The room was made of the same gray stone as the door. A large fire burned across from the door, its light blending with torchlight along the walls. He stepped forward, his footfalls disturbing the silence until he reached the edge of the fire. A faded blue rug lay under his feet. He gazed into the flames. His mind searched for a question he could not quite form. He continued to watch the flames consume the blackening wood. "What am I doing?" a voice whispered, but was pushed back by the crackle of the fire. He leaned until the heat seared his pale skin. His hand reached out against his will, his fingers trailing just above the flames.

Something touched his shoulder. He whirled around to find a tall man standing behind him dressed in the bright blue robes of a defendant. Kyle jerked back, startled. The defendant fell to the ground at his feet.

"Gods!" Kyle exclaimed. Bodies lined the floor behind him, all dressed in the robes of defendants and high ranking guardsmen. Bloodied swords lay beside their fallen masters. Then two tall men came crashing through the stone doorway.

They were garbed in robes of silver and gold. The one with short black hair wore gold and clutched a matching sword, while the blond one wore and carried silver. The two men stood facing each other, swords clutched tightly in their hands. The golden warrior rushed forward, bringing his sword down upon the edge of the silver's. The sound of the clashing blades left Kyle's ears ringing long after the two men had pulled back for a second stroke. The silver blade came low, its edge sweeping toward the golden's right leg. The man in gold twisted, taking several steps back. The silver warrior followed him.

The silver blade flew towards the golden's right. This time the golden warrior engaged, bringing his own sword down upon the silver. The two circled one another and the golden one thrust his sword forward. The man in silver jerked back just in time to prevent the tip of the golden sword from entering his chest. The golden sword again came down upon the silver. The Silver Defendant parried, twisting his blade. The edge of the gold and silver swords slid against each other with a high-pitched sound.

"Stop this!" the man in gold called to the one in silver. "Have there not been enough deaths already?"

"No!" the one in silver replied. "We are still one short."

The blades again flew high in the air before clashing against each other with astounding ferocity. The golden warrior struck left. The silver twisted away. The golden pursued him across the room. Then the Silver Defendant tripped over the body of one of his fallen comrades. He fell to his knees. It was the opening that his opponent had been searching for. The Golden Defendant brought his blade down, gripping the hilt with both hands. The sword came down, slicing into the Silver Defendant's arm. He cried out and a moment later, the golden sword was at the Silver Defendant's throat. "It's over," the golden said to the silver.

The silver stared up from his kneeling position at the blade. "Don't!" Kyle attempted to call out, but no sound came.

He stood frozen as he watched the Golden Defendant hold his blade over the silver. The golden warrior took a step back when the silver grabbed his blade from the floor. He thrust his sword and drove it into the Golden Defendant's stomach. This time it was the golden blade that clattered to the floor as the Silver Defendant wrapped both hands around the blade and twisted with all his strength, turning the blade through more of the Golden Defendant's organs. The Silver Defendant rose to his feet as the golden fell, and pulled his blade from the Golden Defendant's chest. He stood and then brought the sword down again, this time slicing into his dying opponent's neck. Blood splashed through the air, spraying onto the killer's robes.

When the Golden Defendant finally stopped moving, the silver walked towards Kyle, ignoring the bodies that littered the ground at his feet. He stepped to Kyle's left, oblivious to the other man's presence. The Silver Defendant stared into the flames, holding his blood-covered blade before the fire. Kyle attempted to move but still found himself frozen in place.

A deep growl brought the defendant's attention to Kyle's right, bringing his sapphire blue eyes directly in line with Kyle's emerald gaze. They stared at each other for a single moment, when another deep growl caused the defendant to drop down to one knee. "It is done, my lord," the defendant spoke to room of dead men.

"Yes," the deep throated voice replied. Something moved in the shadows, a glint of eyes in the darkness but unlike any Kyle had ever seen before. They were catlike, slanted - sinister. They seemed to emerge from shadows and sent Kyle's heart straight to his throat. Fear gripped him as those eyes moved closer, the growl growing louder.

"Death," the formless figure growled. The flames behind him brightened and leaped to surround the shadow. The figure, surrounded in flames, moved closer, the heat from the fire first warm then searing at they moved closer to him. The fire spread to his silver *robes, burning the material and causing Kyle to scream as they began to seep towards his skin. "Death to those who love you."*

Kyle awoke in his chambers in a cold sweat. He jerked to a seating position, swinging his legs to the edge of the bed. His hands trembled as he fought to force air down into his lungs. He had dreamed of the two men before, but always in the open field with one killing the other with a single strike. Never had they fought inside a building before. But it was that deep, rough voice from the shadows that had his heart pounding relentlessly through his chest.

Death to those who love you. The words echoed through his mind. He stood and walked towards his tall dresser where his silver robes had been folded the night before. He dressed quickly, his hands still trembling. He drew a series of deep breaths to steady himself and grabbed his blade from beside the bed. He did not bother tying it in place, but instead left his room, rushing down the hall toward the doors to the princess' chambers.

Two men stood before the large door. One was a Pink Defendant, Lord Darius, ranked sixth in defendant leadership. He was a tall man with short brown hair and matching eyes. Beside him, also garbed in pink robes, was Brandan, Kyle's longtime teammate.

"Captain," Brandan addressed him by his assigned role as Mary's temporary Captain of the Guard.

Kyle barely paused to acknowledge him as he stepped between the two men and reached for the door. "I need to see her." He pushed the door open without another word.

"Is everything all right?"

Kyle ignored him and entered the chamber beyond. The room was dark, the fire having dimmed to embers hours before. Mary lay on the far side of the room under a thin layer of golden covers. Kyle exhaled a breath he had not realized he'd been holding. He pressed the back of his hand against his forehead and drew a deep breath. He took several steps so that he could see her face, her long dark hair strew across the gold pillows beneath her. Her chest rose and fell at his approach. He again let out a sharp breath. He tried to turn, but found himself frozen beside the bed.

Death., The words trailed across the room.

He forced down several more breaths before he found the strength to turn away, but had barely taken a step when Mary called out his name. He turned back to face her.

"Kyle," she said again. "What is it?"

He tried to speak, but the words would not seem to form upon his lips. Mary pulled herself up, the covers slipping from her body. She wore a satin gown; the thin gold straps clung to the edge of her pale shoulders. "Kyle?"

He stared down at her, unable to hide his fear. His expression was intense, his frame ridged. "Mary, I…" But he did not know what to say.

She slid back on the bed and motioned him to the side. He moved forward, taking a seat on the edge of the bed. He reached and touched the side of her face. Her head tilted to the left. "What happened?" she asked softly.

"I needed…" He swallowed. "I wanted to know that you were all right."

She continued to study him for several long moments. Something in his expression stilled her questions and instead she found herself saying. "I'm fine." She moved her hand to his and pressed his palm more firmly against her cheek. He searched her gaze, then leaned forward and kissed her. There was a wildness in his touch. He drew back and pulled her into his arms. She let him hold her, not needing reason to understand his need. He held her for a long time before he finally slid back.

"I'm sorry," he told her as he began to climb from the bed.

"Wait."

He froze as she drew him back down. He again sat upon the edge of the bed. She traced a finger along his cheek.

"Kyle, talk to me."

'I'm sorry, my lady. I…I had a terrible feeling and I had to make sure that…I had to see you. I'm sorry."

She embraced him, running her hand up and down his back through silver satin. He buried his head against her shoulder until his fear was chased back by her gentle touch. Her hair smelled of lilac and he breathed in the sweet aroma. His pulse slowed to match that of the woman he now clung to. He forced himself to pull back and again attempted to move from the bed.

"No," she said. "Don't go."

He nodded, relief washing over him. However, when she pulled him down to the bed, he froze. "No. It would not be appropriate."

She met his gaze through the darkness. "I don't know what drove you to such fear, but I am not about to let you leave."

"Let me stand guard."

"You haven't slept," she replied. "You're no good to anyone if you don't get some rest."

"I need to go."

She touched his cheek, turning his gaze more directly into hers. "Everything is going to be okay." Mary stood from the bed. "Lie down for me, Kyle. Don't force me to make it an order." He hesitated but decided not to argue, instead leaning down and tentatively placing his head against the golden pillows. She pulled the covers around him as though tucking in a child and sat on the edge of the bed where he had been only moments before. She stroked his hair, pushing back the dark strands. His eyes closed at her touch.

"This isn't right."

"Kyle, I am the golden student and undefeated champion of the Temple of Kale. This is my job."

"You're a princess," he whispered, exhaustion washing over him as quickly as the fear had previously.

"Yes, and yet I seem to have beaten everyone I have ever come up against—including you." She kissed his brow before moving her hand and slipping it into his. After a long moment, his breathing slowed and steadied. "It is my turn to stand watch. Rest, Kyle. I will stay right here."

Mary sat still for a long time after sleep overcame him. Then she rose from the bed and walked to the door, opening it as softly as she could. She emerged into the hallway wearing only her thin gown and turned to face the two men standing before the large door, relieved to see Brandan's familiar face.

"Princess," he said as both men moved to kneel before her.

She motioned for them to rise and turned to the Pink Defendant. "Get Master Jiro. Quietly."

Nicholas did not ask any questions, merely nodded and turned to walk down the silver hall, leaving her alone with Brandan. "Did Kyle say anything to you before he came into the room?"

"No, Your Highness."

Mary paused. "I need to ask something of you."

"I am at your service."

"I would like you to remain on my guard detail for the next few nights. Exclusively on my detail."

Brandan asked no questions. "Of course, my lady."

Mary nodded. "I'm just not sure who to trust right now."

Brandan's pale green eyes met hers briefly before he bowed at the waist. "I am honored to be deemed worthy of such trust, princess." Mary nodded as Brandan again straightened. "May I ask, what is going on?"

"I'm not sure," she replied. The sound of distant footsteps sounded down the hall. A few moments later, Lord Nicholas appeared with the Kolosian master by his side.

"Your Highness," Jiro addressed her.

"Master," she replied. "I am sorry to wake you."

"Not at all. What is going on?"

"I would like for you to stand guard tonight. And for the next few nights as well."

Tension filled his features. "What happened?"

"I can't explain it." she spoke softly. "It's only a feeling. Probably nothing, but…I want to be safe. Will you please do as I ask and we can speak further in the morning?"

"Of course, princess."

Mary nodded. "Thank you." Then she turned and walked back into the room. Kyle was still asleep where she had left him. She stepped quietly and grabbed a robe from where it hung by the door. She wrapped it around her, the thick material fighting the chill of the cool night air. She walked to a chair, thankful for the thick rug that helped to silence her movements as she maneuvered it closer to the bed. She placed the chair by the bed and then grabbed her golden sword from the desk. She placed the blade on the floor beside and took a seat in the chair. She sat in the silence, listening to the steady sound of Kyle's breathing as she wondered what could have possibly put such fear into one of the bravest men she had ever known.

Chapter XXXVI

———⋆⋅☆⋅⋆———

Princess Ameria awoke to a series of knocks. "Come in," she called, pulling the golden sheets from around her as she struggled to her feet. A man dressed in blue robes of the Serenitas Guard entered the room and took a knee before her. "Forgive me, Your Highness, but your grandfather has requested the honor of your company."

"Of course," she replied. "Tell Lord Riccard that I shall join him momentarily." The man rose and left the room, leaving Ameria to dress into her golden attire. She wore a long-sleeved shirt of gold satin, cinched tightly at the wrist. Over it, she slipped a matching robe that reached her ankles and hung loosely over her arms, the sleeves cut from her wrists. She pulled her golden hair from the inside of the satin, allowing it to cascade down her back in soft waves. She ran a brush through the golden locks as her eyes trailed again to the large collection of trophies standing before the mirror.

She picked up the one closest to her right. *Tournament of Desoto Royal Championship: Lady Annabelle and Lord Jiro of Koloso.* She traced her fingers over the engraving before placing it back on the desk and picked up the one beside it. "Tournament of Kevera," she read aloud. Yet here, she could not make out the name. She blew on the thin layer of dust, running her thumb over the gold. *Tournament of Koloso* appeared as did *Lady...* But the rest of the name was gone, smooth to the touch as though the engraving had never existed. She grabbed the next trophy with her left hand for comparison and found that it clearly stated, *Tournament of Kale Royal Championship: Lady Annabelle and Lord Jiro of Koloso.* She placed the second trophy back where she had found it and again glanced at the one in her right hand. How strange that the name was unreadable while it stood so clearly against the other words. She reached for the next one when another knock at her door stole her attention.

"My lady," Lord Stephen called. "I am to escort you to Lord Riccard."

"Yes," she answered, placing the trophy back to where it belonged before walking briskly towards the door. Stephen stood awaiting her in clothing identical to her own, save for the silver color. Ameria paused to study the older man for several moments, noting how his brown hair was beginning to show a touch of gray, more a sign of distinguishment than age. He bowed to the waist awaiting her permission to rise. Yet Ameria seemed to stand silently for a long time, her eyes tracing along the outline of his shimmering robes.

"Tell me, Lord Stephen. How does it feel to know that, no matter what the outcome of this fight, you will never wear the golden robes?"

He remained silent, by now used to hearing such abusive questions from the princess and was surprised when she said, "Look at me." He rose to comply, fighting to keep annoyance from his features, however, her expression caused him to focus his view more fully upon her. "I do not ask in jest or cruelty, my lord. I genuinely want to know—how does it feel?"

"Why does it matter?"

"Because I asked and as your princess, you are bound to answer."

"My lady, I…"

"Honesty, Stephen. Only honesty will do."

He paused in unspoken acknowledgment of her warning. "Frustrating," he stated. "And more than that. It is…difficult to put into words."

"Try."

"To be trained for something all your life and finally have it within your grasp, knowing it will never be yours after you have devoted your entire life to obtaining it? You truly want to know how that feels? To know what is yours by right—what you earned—is to be given to another?" He drew a deep, breath gazing into her deep blue eyes. "I will answer your question, Your Highness, when you answer one of mine. Tell me how it feels to see your sister upon the throne guarded by the man who, more than any other, should be by your side? Tell me that, princess, and know my answer."

Her thoughts flew to Kyle; the touch of gentleness that filled his voice when he spoke to her sister. The way he looked at her. A look of protectiveness and caring that Ameria had never seen grace his face for her. Her sister had been named heir to the throne by their uncle, trained in the highest of all the temples…must she possess Kyle's heart as well? She felt her hand tighten its grip on the hilt of her silver blade—the same once carried by Lord Kale himself—but did not draw it from its place at her side.

She studied Stephen intently, then answered. "Tell me this. Is it an agony with which you can live? Is that anger, so raw and real, a tool or a hindrance? A power or a weakness?" She took a step towards him, her eyes searching his. "Can I trust you, Lord Stephen?" He could feel her warm breath against his skin. "To truly be silver to my gold? Partner to my leadership? To place my life into your keeping?" Her left hand touched his cheek and the caress seemed to intimate for the coldness in her voice—the dangerous intensity in her gaze. "Can I trust you? Or will that agony that shines through your eyes tear this realm apart?"

He wanted to answer, yet no words seemed to come. "You need not answer now," she traced a single finger down his cheek. "But the day will soon come and on that day—I expect nothing less than the truth." She stepped back, pulling away from the Silver Defendant before turning down the long stone corridor. "Come," she commanded. "Lord Riccard awaits."

Chapter XXXVII

◆━❧✦❧━◆

Morning light filtered through the tall window long before Kyle awoke. He opened his eyes, a sense of peace that he had not felt in ages running through him as the sunlight splashed the large room with an array of colors that sparkled off the golden satin he lay upon.

Wait. His mind slowly processed his surroundings. *Golden?* He turned, raising himself from the mattress as he realized that he was in Mary's chambers. Memories from the previous night returned in a wave of realization as he rose from the bed. "Princess."

Mary sat in a large chair covered with thick cushions. Her golden robe was tied around her with a thick satin sash and her sword lay on the floor to the right of the chair. "Good morning."

"My lady." He slid to the edge of bed, swinging his legs over the side. "I'm—" His words came fast and unsteady. "I'm sorry. I don't know what came over me." He started to stand when Mary stood and guided him back down to the bed.

"It's all right." Her words were calm, reassuring. "Everything is all right."

He looked into her emerald eyes. "I can't believe that I came here. That I disturbed you like this. I am so sorry."

"Calm down," she cut through his ranting as she took a knee before him.

"I'm sorry," he said again.

She shook her head, motioning him to silence. "You have nothing to be sorry for." She took his hand in her own. "It's alright. Talk to me, Kyle. Tell me what happened."

"I panicked. I have no excuse. I…"

"Kyle," she interrupted. "Talk to me as if I were not a princess."

"But you are a princess. You're my princess."

"Not right now," she replied. "Right now I am the Golden Student of Kale. Your teammate, your friend, gold to your silver. I need you to talk to me. Tell me what happened."

"I…I had this dream. This nightmare. It was…" He shook his head before returning his gaze to hers.

"And you don't think I would understand that?" She reached a hand up and caressed the left side of his face. "How many nightmares have you pulled me from, since this all began? How many fits of madness have you saved me from?" She shook her head. "Gods, Kyle. You think you have to be sorry for this? There is nothing, do you hear me, nothing to be sorry for."

He shook he head. "I am your captain."

"Yes, but I am also yours. Sometimes I think your forget who I am. I am not a dainty princess. I am not helpless. I am a daughter of Kale, trained at the highest temple in the land and an undefeated champion of that temple; Master Leo's chosen heir." She drew a deep breath. "I know that these have been hard months. I know I have scared you and for that, I am sorry. But Kyle, please. Do not treat me as less than I am."

He stared at her for a long moment and then finally nodded. "Okay."

She rose from her knees and took a seat beside him on the edge of the bed. "I need you to know that you can always come to me. Tell me you know this. Promise me that you will."

"Okay." He nodded, grasping her hands in his own. "I promise."

She nodded, the tension easing from her taut frame.

"I needed to see you. I had a feeling I could not shake. I do not know how else to explain it." He drew a deep breath and shook his head. "I should have added more guards."

"I did," she replied. "Master Jiro is standing watch."

"Good." Kyle let out a breath he had not realized he had been holding. "That's good."

She moved her hand back to his cheek, pressing the back of her hand against his skin. "Take a breath, Kyle." He complied, closing his eyes at the gentleness of her touch. "We will get through this. I don't know how, but," she searched for the words, "we must find the faith. In fact…" She suddenly stood from the bed, pulling him with her. "Come with me."

He did not question, merely followed as she walked across the large room and opened the doors to her chambers. Guarding the entrance stood Master Jiro in the silver robes of Koloso and Brandan in pink. "Princess." Jiro bowed his head as Mary emerged while Brandan took a knee.

"Follow us," she instructed before moving between the two men, then held her arm out to Kyle. He stepped forward and wrapped his arm around her own, walking silently down the hall with the two additional Kolosians trailing a few steps behind them. She led the group to the west side of the place grounds and emerged into the full light of all three Kalian suns. They walked down a series of marble stairs and down a matching pathway that had been carved into the bright blue grass. They did not have to walk far before they reached the tall, marble structure which towered above them.

Large white columns lined the entrance, supporting the domed ceiling that rose high above the group. "Stay here," Mary instructed the two men behind her. "We will enter the temple alone." The building had been in serious need of repair when Mary had become acting queen. One of her first royal decrees had been to restore the temple and the statues within to their former glory. Repairs had been commissioned around the clock for several months as the statues were gathered from the far corners of the palace grounds and returned to their rightful places. Mary ascended the wide stairs. There were no doors to the temple, but instead a large golden gate which was opened by the guards stationed there.

They entered the temple alone and walked to the fountain standing in its center. Identical to the statues standing before the Temples of Koloso and Kale, the statue of dark and light towered over the two champions. The statues were of a pair of golden horses with jeweled eyes. One of the horses had eyes of diamonds, while the other's eyes were of a black crystal. The two horses of dark and light stood high, their hooves pawing the air, nostrils flared. Mary continued walking, the frozen eyes seeming to beckon to her. The silent reverence with which the two champions approached the guardians was disturbed only by the water, which ran in rainbow streams from the horses' mouths, splashing into the base of the fountain below and the echo of Mary's heels as they struck the marble floor.

Mary knelt before the guardians while Kyle shadowed her movements. "May the Gods of Kale and Koloso hear my prayer," she spoke firmly, projecting her voice to fill the temple. "I, Princess Mariana of the Kalian bloodline, golden student of the temples and Champion of the Kalian Tournaments, and Lord Kyle, heir to the Province of Turbantemum, silver student of the temples and Champion of the Kalian Tournaments, call upon you—hear our prayer. Grant us the wisdom to know what is right and the courage to carry out the fate you have bequeathed with the grace and skill of those who came before. Shelter and protect those we love in these dark times. Guide us, oh Gods above, to lead your followers with the wisdom and fortitude to withstand all adversity which you see fit to bestow. I ask this, oh Gods above, in the name of your honor and the glory of your temples."

Mary lay down upon the white marble under her, stretching her hands out in front of her so that her palms lay flat against the ground. She lay there for several long moments before rising to her feet. She walked to the right side of the statue. There, a few inches shorter than her, stood a pillar of stone far darker than the pale marble surrounding it. In the center of this pillar sat a large crystal bowl between two flat pieces of stone. Mary bowed as she reached the edge of the pillar and then stepped forward. On the left side of the crystal was a small, silver knife lying atop a piece of black cloth. Mary grasped the sacrificial blade in the palm of her right hand and then proceeded to run the sharp edge along the palm of her left hand. The sharp tip sliced easily into her skin. She suppressed a hiss, instead enduring the sharp sting in silence as blood began to rise to the surface. She then moved her hand over the blessed water within the shimmering crystal and watched her royal blood slowly mix with that of the Gods above.

Chapter XXXVIII

Ameria walked briskly down the hall, but paused when she came to the edge of one of the grand entryways. A masculine voice carried down the hallway, distracting the princess from her path. "My lord, I have come for assistance."

"You may speak," came another voice. This one she recognized as belonging to her uncle.

"The village is refusing to supply the soldiers with food, as is required in exchange for protection."

Ameria peered around the corner. Along the far back wall her uncle sat in her grandfather's silver chair atop a set of stone steps. He wore the dark blue robes of Serenitas. Beside him stood Lord Karris, who was by all delivered accounts, a pet of her uncle's. As he had never attended a temple, he was not permitted to wear the robes donned by her uncle, and instead wore a pair of dark slacks and a long-sleeved black shirt with silver buttons.

They stood facing a small crowd. At the center was a man who Ameria guessed was another lower-ranking lord. His attire was similar to Karris', except for the color of his shirt, which was pale green. He had shoulder-length blond hair. Beside him stood a woman clearly of lower standing, given her simple, pale blue gown and her tanned skin, likely darkened from spending a lifetime working outdoors. She had plain brown hair that reached just past her shoulders, and from her limited view, looked uncomfortable standing between the higher-ranked men.

"This woman," the man continued speaking, "is the one leading the village to refuse our soldiers. We already stopped collecting taxes, now this as well? Are we, your most loyal of lords to be made destitute after all we have done for this kingdom?"

Ameria slid back, hiding herself from view as she awaited her uncle's response.

"The choice to cut the taxes did not come from me, as well you know, Lord Lucious."

"I know that!" he replied crossly. "But come now, we changed the laws from money to food, as per our requirement."

Andrew turned his eyes upon the woman standing beside the lower lord. "Is this true? Are you refusing to pay the men their portions of the yearly yield?"

The woman took a step closer. "My lord, it is not that I want to disobey. But there is barely enough food in the village for ourselves. With some families there isn't enough, period."

"Why is that?" Andrew demanded. "Was there a problem with the summer harvest?"

"No, my lord. The food was harvested. But, well, you see, it's the raids. We are on the border lands and the raiders have come through several times and taken the majority of what we had stored. Along with other things. My sister had her jewels taken, the ones left to her by my great-grandmother. They are—"

"You demand protection," Lord Lucious stated. "How can we offer such when you refuse to provide for the men?" He shook his head. "I have told you there will be no more protection until you comply with my demands."

"My lord," the woman pleaded, directing her words not at Lucious but at Andrew. "If we feed the soldiers, we will starve." Ameria again snuck a glance, and saw that the woman had fallen to her knees upon the stone floor. "Please," she said again.

"I think that we should…"

"My lord," Karris spoke from his place on Andrew's right. "May I have a moment?"

Ameria watched as Karris leaned and whispered for Andrew's ears alone. After several moments, the son of the high lord gave a silent nod and then turned back towards the pleading woman. "The law states that these men are entitled to half of your yearly harvest. A few months ago, you were also required to pay taxes. Your pleas were heard and you now pay no more alms to the crown. The loss of these fees means that the men who serve this realm, who protect it, must be paid in other ways. Now you are saying that you cannot give the food as well?"

Ameria felt her eyes narrowing. It had been her sister who had ordered a stop to the unlawful taxing of the people, not the lords.

"My lord, if we give the food to the soldiers, our people will surely starve. You cannot ask us to give what we do not have."

"They have the food," Lucious stated. "They simply do not want to comply with the law. Greedy is what they are. Ungrateful peasants showing nothing but disrespect to their rightful lords."

"Please," the woman called desperately. "My lord I mean no disrespect to anyone. We need help, please."

"The high lord has spoken," Karris said. "You will comply with the law. Anyone who does not will be imprisoned."

"My lord—"

"Silence," Karris stated. "Remove that woman from these chambers."

Ameria had heard enough. She stepped from the corner and entered the room, the sound of her heels echoing against the stone. Lucious turned and at the sight of her robes, sank to his knees beside the distraught woman. "Your Highness," the lord stated.

She walked towards the man and paused a few paces from him, her eyes scanning the room towards where both her uncle and Karris had moved to the edge of the stairs before falling to their knees as well. "Princess," Andrew addressed her.

She purposely allowed the room to fill with silence for several moments before turning her gaze upon her uncle's kneeling form. "Tell me," she spoke carefully emphasizing the pronunciation of each syllable. "Did I hear correctly, that you just ordered this woman to pay half of her village's harvest to the soldiers of this," she motioned to Lucious, "man?"

The silence continued until Lord Karris cleared his throat. "Your Highness."

"Was I speaking to you?" she demanded in an icy tone. She turned back to where Lord Stephen stood. "Tell me, Silver Defendant, was I speaking to him?"

"No, my princess."

"Then why does he speak?" She turned back towards the two men. "You had best learn to control your advisor, uncle. Otherwise I am afraid I might be forced to allow Lord Stephen to do so for you." She drew a deep breath. "Now answer my question, Lord Andrew. Did I hear correctly that you intend to force these poor villagers to pay the price for your soldiers' inability to protect them…or not?"

"My princess," Andrew stated. "It is the law of the land that the villagers help feed the soldiers."

"Yes," she replied. "And pray, do tell, what do the villagers receive in return?"

"Why, they are the soldiers—"

"I do not like repeating myself. Yet I find myself asking again: what do the villagers receive in return?"

"Why, protection, of course."

"Ah, yes. Protection." She gave a nod as a scowl began to crawl over her features. "Then tell me, my lord. Please, do explain. If the villages are receiving protection in exchange for the food they provide…" Her uncle looked up but did not reply. "Very well, I will be more specific. If the solders are protecting the villages, then why, do tell, was half of the harvest stolen by raiders?"

"I…"

"You are trying my patience."

"It is the first I am hearing of it, my lady."

"The first you are hearing of it?" she stated in disbelief.

"Yes."

"And yet, you show no concern over the fact that there are thieves riding throughout your province? Raiding your villages? Stealing from the people you are sworn to protect as their rightful lords?"

"I…"

"Yes, 'I' would be the problem. It is always 'I' with you. Never the people. Never those you serve. I had heard that about you, Lord Andrew. But I failed to believe it until this moment. This woman comes to inform you that raiders are stealing from your people and instead of offering her aide, you instead propose further harm. You should be ashamed to call yourself the son of a high lord."

"Your Highness…"

"I did not give you leave to speak!" She again turned back to the Silver Defendant. "Why does everyone keep speaking without permission? Have these lands forgotten how to treat their rightful rulers?" She turned back to Andrew. "I am your princess. The next time you forget this fact, may very well be your last. This woman has come to you for help. What will you do?"

Yet, it was Karris who spoke, though more cautiously than before. "My princess, may I have permission to speak?" Ameria's eyes simmered as they shifted to the lower-ranked lord but she nodded her consent. "My lady, those lands are on the outer borders. They are the farthest away from the safety provided by the Rainbow Mountains. It is a dangerous area and has been for some time. It would be unfair to expect Lord Lucious to drive out the invaders."

Ameria considered this for a moment. "So to be clear, Lord Karris, I understand by your statement that you were, in fact, aware of the problems occurring in Lucious' province, and failed to report such knowledge to your high lord? As my uncle proclaims to have no previous knowledge of these raids. Is that correct?" It was Karris' turn to fall silent, causing

Ameria to turn her attention back to her uncle. "Are you saying that you, the most powerful lord in the kingdom, a former defendant and a Royal Champion of Kale, cannot defend his people from a group of bandits? That you would force your people to starve?" She shook her head. "You should be ashamed to call yourself my grandfather's heir."

She turned from them then and faced the woman still kneeling on the floor at her feet. "Arise, my lady," she instructed and watched the woman climb slowly to her feet. "Do you know who I am?"

The woman stared at her for several moments and finally said, "The Kolosian princess?"

"Yes. And as your princess I give you my word, that your village will be protected from this point forward. In fact, Karris," she turned back to face him, "since you seem to have such little faith in Lucious' ability to provide adequate protection to his people, I am placing you, personally, in charge of ensuring their safety."

"Me?" His gaze snapped up from the floor.

"Of course. Unless you feel that you are unable to honor the most basic of commitments required of every Kalian lord?"

"I…"

"Stand up."

He climbed clumsily to his feet and met her gaze.

"You will lead their protection detail yourself. You will ensure these raids are stopped. If I hear that so much as a single grain of rice has been stolen, I will personally have your stripped of every privilege to which you have ever thought yourself entitled and have you thrown into the palace towers. Do you understand me, Karris?"

He stared at her with his first taste of fear. "I understand, Your Highness."

Ameria nodded before turning back towards the woman. "In two months' time I will personally send the Silver Defendant to visit your village. You will report to him all that has occurred between now and then. If these soldiers have violated your rights or stolen goods in any way, or if Karris has failed to stop the raids, I shall remove both him and Lucious from power and send the defendants to correct their failures."

"Thank you, princess. Thank you."

"You need not thank me for fulfilling my duty to the kingdom." She nodded and turned again to Karris. "Oh yes, and one more thing, my lord. Should anything happen to this woman or should she be 'suddenly' unavailable to speak to the defendants, I will not merely strip you of your title, but of your life as well. Am I understood?"

Silence extended into a small eternity this time and Ameria finally said, "I will take it by your silence that I am." She turned to face the door and saw who the others in the room had glimpsed before she did.

"Lord Riccard," she addressed her grandfather. "Forgive my delay. I understand you wished to see me."

"Yes," Riccard replied, motioning her to his side. "I was planning to attend morning prayers and wanted to know if you wished to accompany me."

Ameria offered a slight bow. "Certainly, Grandfather. I would be honored."

Riccard shot a glance towards his son, who had still not been given permission to rise, but did not acknowledge him beyond the disapproving glance. Ameria moved across the floor and slid her arm around her grandfather's. They walked together with steady steps across the stone floor with the Silver Defendant trailing a few paces behind.

Chapter XXXIX

After that night, Kyle's chambers were moved to those closest to the princess. Mary attempted to keep a respectful distance from the man serving as her captain, however it was difficult. The act of being so close to him, and yet so distant caused an ache deep inside of her chest. He was always there by her side, whether it was walking through the halls of the palace or seated upon the silver throne which Mary was beginning to believe would never feel like her own. She had begun to allow Lord Chiro to take over more matters of state, which allowed her more time to prepare for the upcoming thirteenth tournament.

The fight for the throne loomed and Mary began to train each afternoon to the point of sheer exhaustion. These moments were the only ones in which Kyle was not with her, as he forced himself to refrain from again stepping upon the golden mats to face her. Instead it was Lord Jiro who oversaw her training and came to be her constant companion and competitor within the ring. What the temple master lacked in youth, he compensated for with a lifetime of skill and training. His style was far different from the master she had spent her life training under as Jiro was more cautious in his attacks that Master Leo had ever been. A part of her could not help but wonder if it had been Jiro who stood between Alec and the palace gates, if the battle might have had a different outcome?

These were thoughts which she worked to push from her mind as she turned to face off against the temple master until one night, after exhaustion had all but claimed them both, she sat down upon the golden mats. Breathing heavily, she was handed a large glass of water by one of the servants and drank deeply. When she was finally able to again draw a steady breath, she gazed up at Jiro from her seated position. "May I ask you something, master?"

"Of course." He lowered himself down on the silver side of the mat as he was handed his own glass of water by one of the palace servants.

"I want to know, and it is my understanding that you do not know the answer. However, you were there and I was…"

"I will do my best to answer any question you may have, my lady."

"My mother has told me a great many stories about the past. Particularly pertaining to the life of Alec's and Ryan's father." She shifted to better look into Jiro's green eyes. "Do you believe that he did it? Did he kill my father's love? And…" She had to fight down the urge to reject the vile words. "Did Leo order her death?"

Jiro drew a deep, slow breath. "My lady…I…" He paused attempting to find the correct words. "My princess, you must understand that the kingdom was on the brink of war." He shook his head. "I have seen a lot of battle in my time, my lady. But that one, was by far the worst. It threatened to tear the very fabric of the kingdom apart. It was fought far from the healing chambers of any temple. I spent the better part of two days killing those scattered across the field who would not be able to survive."

Mary nodded, sliding across the mat to place herself closer to Jiro's side. "I am not here to judge the battle or the actions required by those who were forced to partake. I only ask if, to the best of your knowledge and opinion, did Master Leo order the death of a fellow defendant?"

"Master Leo loved you, Mariana. And what happened in the past is better left where it lies."

"But Jiro, it is not in the past. It walked through the doors of this palace with a sword in its hand and cut down by those who believe they were deprived of their honorable birthright. It killed my father. I need to know if you believe it?"

Jiro eyed her for a long moment before attempting to answer. "I have asked myself that very question a thousand times over the years, my lady. Nathan was my friend, an upper-level defendant to whom I would have trusted him with my life without question. The thought of him killing another defendant was unthinkable—it is still unthinkable. But, my lady…I do not know if it is implausible as well. Nathan was a practical enough man to realize that your father would never be able to abandon the woman he loved—not even for the fate of the kingdom. His refusal would have resulted in many more battles and countless lives lost." He drew a deep breath. "Oh, I do not doubt that your grandfather would have been victorious in the end. The king was a fool with no temple training and no loyalty among the defendants. Your grandfather was a former Golden Defendant with years of training in battle. There was no question of who the victor would be; merely the number of lives it cost to achieve such victory. Sometimes I…"

"Sometimes what?"

"Forgive me, princess. I speak out of turn."

"No, go ahead and say it."

Jiro shifted uncomfortably. "It is unwise to speak ill of the dead."

"Say it anyway. I will not hold anything you say against you, Master. You have my word."

Jiro studied her for several moments before speaking. "Sometimes, Your Highness, I wonder if things would have turned out differently had the war been fought, and your father placed upon the throne. If you had been born the heir instead of the niece of the king. The battle was brutal and lives would have been lost. However, I cannot help but wonder if we did not pay a far greater price under the rule of a man who knew nothing of the temples. Your grandfather was so adamant that bad things would follow, should the vow of Blood and Arms be broken." He shook his head. "Sometimes, I wonder if the price would have been worth the outcome. I wish I could say with certainty, but…"

She nodded. "I understand," she spoke softly. "You are not the first to offer such thoughts. However, please, my lord. Will you answer my question? Did Leo order the death of my father's love?"

Jiro gave a deep sigh and gazed into Mary's emerald eyes. "I don't know anything for certain, my lady. However, I can say this. The events of that battle haunt me. Its violence, its ability to pit friends one against the other. The threat of splitting the kingdom. Master Leonardo of Kale was an intelligent, powerful and practical man, in many ways far more Kolosian than Kalian. I do not know what he ordered or did not order that day and I do not know if either he or Nathan were involved in the lady's death. What I can tell, is this." He continued to hold her gaze. "Had I been the Golden Defendant that day, I would have committed whatever acts necessarily to ensure that no further battles were to come. Even if that meant ending the life of the woman my best friend loved more than the kingdom to which he had sworn his very soul." He drew a deep breath. "I do not know if that is the answer you were seeking. However I fear it is the only answer I am able to give."

"So it is possible then. Nathan might have followed orders." She cringed, but forced herself to speak the words. "Leo's orders to kill Lillian. And been exiled for carrying out those orders. It is possible."

"The only ones who truly know the answer to that question, was Leo himself."

"Did Nathan protest his innocence?"

"He stated that they were attacked on the road and Lilian incurred additional injuries on the journey. However…I don't know, my lady. I wish I could give you the answers you seek. But, I am afraid that I cannot."

She nodded. "I thank you for your candor, Master."

"May I be so bold, princess, to ask you something as well?"

"Of course."

"If Leo did order Lilian's death. If Nathan was simply following orders. If his children were, in fact, denied the birthright that was rightfully theirs and forced into exile wrongly by the prince and the temple master—what will you do?"

She drew a breath and closed her eyes in a desperate attempt to clear her head. Instead she was returned to the memory of Leo dying before her eyes. Stabbed through the side, the blade having slipped expertly through his ribs, exposing his lungs to the naked eye. His breaths rose in harsh, wheezing gasps. Her hands held tightly to the torn strips of her golden robe which she had tied in vain around his side, pulling the silk as tightly as she could as the material transformed from shimmering gold to blood red before her eyes. *Please, Leo*, she had pleaded. *You're the only real father I have ever known. I can't do this without you.* She had put her face on his chest, begging him to live even as she felt his heart stop beating.

I love you, Mariana. His words haunted her memory. *You were the daughter I never had.*

She opened her eyes to stare into Jiro's, so like the master who had died in her arms. Darkness stirred deep within her as the words rose forth and spilled from her lips. "It does not matter how they were wronged or what birthright denied them. They killed the Temple Master of Kale. They killed the Crown Prince of the Realm. They killed the Golden Defendant. They have to be stopped. The good of the kingdom depends upon it." Jiro studied the young woman, the anger in her eyes and the pain of Leo's death again a fresh anguish over her features. "What is it?" she asked, unable to hide the anger from her words.

"I was only observing, my lady."

"What?"

"That you have never looked more like your sister, than in this moment."

His words fueled her anger. "He was my father."

"Which one, my lady? Leo or the prince?"

She stood from the mat, pulling her golden blade from the ground and placing it back into the sheath at her side. "Does it matter? He killed them both." She turned to leave the room, but paused at the sound of Jiro's voice.

"My princess," he called. She turned back to face him, her hand clutching tightly to her sword. "If you wish to take this quest of vengeance, then I am ready to swear my loyalty to you, Mariana—unto death."

She stared at him for several moments standing tall in his long, silver robes. "Then may the temple Gods hear our prayer, master. For it may very well come to that." He offered a low bow as she turned to leave the room. She walked faster than she would have liked.

Standing upon the mat closest to the golden doors, Kyle stood speaking with Brandan. Both moved to follow her, but had to rush to match her pace. "My lady," Kyle called.

She did not answer him, but continued to walk toward her chambers, her mind jumbled from the visceral memory. She turned down several long corridors with the two Kolosians never more than a pace behind her. "My lady," Kyle stated again as she reached the entrance to her chambers.

"Guard the door," she replied. She pulled on the golden handle and closed it behind her, and walked across the room to the bed. Leo had been more than her master. He had been the father her own had never been as well as her friend, her confidant, the one she trusted most. Could it really be after everything Leo had seen her through, that she had not known him at all? Had he been the loving father she remembered, or this political, cold man that others seemed to be describing? She found herself suddenly questioning every kind word, every gentle encouragement that had eventually lead her down the path upon which she now traveled.

She found herself reflecting on the argument they had the day her uncle had called her to court. *"I think this is what we have been waiting for,"* Leo had stated. *"At long last, the king will be forced to declare you his heir."*

"His heir?" she had asked. *"But Leo, I…"* She drew a breath in an attempt to gather her words. *"I know nothing about the courts. I want to be a temple master, like you."*

Leo shook his head. *"I am sorry, Mary. But you always knew that there was a possibility that you might become queen one day."*

"Well yes, but I…" She shook her head. *"I know nothing about being queen."*

"You will learn."

"But Leo…"

"It is what we have been hoping for. At long last the throne returned to a child of the temples, as it was always meant to be."

"Leo, no. Surely there must be someone else. My sister is royal as well. Perhaps she would prefer…"

"A Kolosian queen," Leo stated with a sharp edge to his voice that she had rarely heard. *"You know that the Temple of Kale would never permit such an atrocity. You should be ashamed to even suggest such a thing."*

Mary's gaze trailed to the floor, heat rising to her cheeks. "I'm sorry. But, Leo…" She shook her head. "Is it not enough that I wish to someday take your place here at the temple? To lead this temple as you have done?"

Leo's jade green eyes looked at her with such sadness. "You know I would be proud to see you in my position someday, my lady. But you are a princess and have a duty to reunite the temples with your crown. It is what is required of you, my princess. By the laws of man and the Gods above."

"Leo, please. I…I don't want to be queen. I want to stay here. To fight, to be a part of this tradition for which I have trained for so long. Please, Leo."

"Mariana." He used her rarely spoken full name, taking a step closer to where she stood. He grasped her chin between his fingers, forcing her gaze up to meet his own. "You will do your duty to this kingdom, Mariana. You will honor the Gods and restore their names to the king's forsaken realm."

"Leo, please…"

"No." His voice was firm, almost harsh. "You will be named your uncle's heir and once you do, you will kneel down before the entire court and swear yourself to the ancient oath of Blood and Arms. Do you understand, Mariana?"

"Yes," she answered. "Forgive me."

He studied her for several more moments then leaned and placed a kiss upon her right cheek before pulling her into an embrace. "I am sorry, Mary. But this is how it must be."

Now, only a few months later, she was attempting in vain to sit upon the most coveted of thrones. "Leo," she whispered. "Gods I wish you were here. I am so lost without your guidance."

You must reunite the temples to the ancient bloodline. His words echoed again. *You are a princess.*

"Don't you think I know that!" she spoke aloud as though she could argue with the memories which plagued her. "Don't you think I know!" Anger rushed through her and tears began to sting her eyes. "You were supposed to be here! You were supposed to tell me how to do this! I am not a queen. I am not…I…"

She drew a shaking breath when she heard the faint echo of the most painful of words he had ever spoken. *What a Golden Defendant you would make.* He had whispered upon his last breath.

"What do you mean?" she asked the man who would never again answer. "What in the name of all the Gods is that supposed to mean? You forced me to be the queen! You made me do this! You…" She reached for the nearest object, a small glass of water sitting on the table beside the bed. She picked it up and threw it across the room with a sharp yell of frustration. The glass hit the far wall, shattering with a loud clash that caused the door to her bedroom to fly open, Kyle rushing in with his naked blade in his hand.

Mary buried her face into her hands as Kyle walked towards her. "Princess, are you all right?"

She drew several deep breaths before raising her gaze and turning towards him. "I'm sorry," she said. "I didn't mean to…I'm sorry."

"Are you all right?"

"Yes. No. I…" She shook her head and ran her fingers through her long dark hair. "*Sutis*!" she cursed.

He returned the blade to his side and walked closer to where she was seated upon the edge of the golden blankets. "My lady," he stated. "What happened?"

"Nothing…everything. I…" She forced herself to look up at him. "I miss Leo," she confessed. "I was so sure of everything with him here. But now, I…I have so many questions and there are no answers. I am supposed to be a queen. A queen should have the answers. I…" She shook her head. "I'm sorry."

"It is okay, my lady. We will find a way to get through this."

She nodded, suddenly exhausted. "I know. I am sorry." She glanced at the broken shards of glass scattered across the floor. "I made a mess."

"Don't worry, I will take care of it."

She nodded and lay down atop the golden blankets, not bothering to pull them over her. Turning away from Kyle, she closed her eyes and listened to the sound of him removing the broken glass from the floor. His mere presence comforted her as she drifted off to sleep.

Yet even Kyle could not guard her from her dreams.

Chapter XL

Kyle cleaned up the glass as best he could, making a mental note to have the floor more thoroughly swept the next morning. Mary's breathing reached the gentle rhythm of sleep long before he was done. She was training herself past the point of exhaustion and had visibly lost weight over the previous few weeks. He watched her with Master Jiro from afar. She fought with a ferocity that he had never before seen within the Kalian princess, though what she was fighting, he was uncertain. He stood against the back wall for several moments, watching her breathe. He longed to take away her pain. A part of him desperately wondered if it was too late to take her away from this. If he could sweep her into his arms and carry her…

Nonsense. He shook his head before turning and leaving the room as quietly as he could so not to wake her. Brandan stood at his usual post, however Kyle was surprised to find that the man next to him was not a member of the normal guard, but instead his father. The high lord stood tall in his silver robes, a blade tucked securely against his side. "Father," Kyle stated after softly closing the door to Mary's chambers.

"Walk with me," his father instructed, turning towards the long corridor.

"The princess…"

"Has plenty of guards," Chiro stated. "I will not keep you long."

Kyle relented and followed his father down a series of long hallways before entering a large, isolated sitting room with a large fire along the left wall. "Have a seat, Kyle." His father motioned to one of the two red sofas on the far side of the wall. Kyle moved, seating himself on the cushion closest to the fire as his father moved to take a seat across from him. Chiro drew a deep breath before speaking. "I understand that you have moved your chambers to those beside the princess?"

"Yes."

"Is there any particular reason why?"

"I am the captain of her guard. It is my duty to be as close to her as possible."

Chiro eyed him critically. "And is it also your duty, my son, to stay in her room?"

Kyle felt his body tense. "I...I made a mistake that night."

"Did you sleep with her, Kyle?"

"That is none of your business."

"Yes, it is. She rules this land as will any child she bears. That makes it my business, Kyle. It makes it the business of the entire kingdom."

"Do you honestly have to ask me such a question?" Anger began to fuel his voice. "Do you think so little of me as to believe I would besmirch her honor so carelessly?"

"No. But I would be remiss if I did not, yet again, remind you of your duties to your family, your temple, and your queen."

"My queen?"

"You are sworn to protect her."

"From what?" he demanded.

"From herself, Kyle!" His father shook his head, a deep sigh filling the room.

"This isn't fair. This oath, these promises. The traditions. She is young. She shouldn't have to be in charge of all of this. She wasn't raised to be a queen."

"No," Chiro answered sharply. "She was born one. As you were born to be a high lord and Ameria was born to be a princess. This is not a question of learning to become something or choosing a particular path. She was born royalty. She can spend her entire life running, hiding, denying the truth - but she cannot escape what she is any more than you can."

Kyle stared at his father for a long time. "She is the most beautiful, graceful, woman I have ever known. And I...I have never seen her this unhappy."

"It is of love you speak, Kyle. I understand it. You are young—you both are. However, I need you to heed my words. She is of a royal, ancient and unbroken bloodline. In our land, under our laws, and by the rule of our Gods, her destiny was spoken for long before she drew her first breath. It is not an easy destiny. But the sentiments of which you speak, those of love, and yes, even of happiness, are the fairytales of lesser men. They are the stories we tell the people, the comforts we offer in order to keep them from desiring more extraordinary lives." He shook his head. "It is rare enough among the upper levels of the lords. But among royalty? Never."

"I refuse to believe that. That cannot be the way."

"It is the way it has always been." Chiro stood and walked to where his son was sitting on the couch. He lightly squeezed Kyle's left shoulder. "I am not going to tell you what to do, Kyle. I am merely going to tell you that with the Crown Princess you are on dangerous ground."

"Dangerous ground?"

"Yes. There is something…dark, which watches over the royal family. And it has taken particular interest in these young girls who vie for the throne. Did it never occur to you, Kyle, to wonder why you did not die when you stepped between their blades? They called on the Gods, but tell me this. What kind of Gods spare one life, at the cost of another?" He stared directly into his son's eyes. "Beware the wrath of the Gods, Kyle. They will come for the Twins of Kale." With those words, his father turned and left the room, leaving him alone with the soft crackling of the fire.

His mind wandered to his dreams. The formless terror that haunted his sleepless nights, moving in the dark. Whispering though shadow. A chill ran through him and he rose from the cushions to stand closer to the fire, holding his pale hands toward their offered embrace. "I want to keep her safe," he whispered to the encroaching darkness. "Please, Gods above, help me keep her safe."

From the back of the room, the wraith watched in silence.

Chapter XLI

MARY SAT ON THE EDGE of the silver throne, staring down upon the men standing before her. Chiro had taken over the majority of these meetings, however he had insisted on her attending to a few matters herself. She had first addressed a dispute between two neighboring lords, who were arguing over the possession of a castle which lay between the boarders of their lands. She had eventually declared that the high lord of the land would go assess the property. Then she dealt with a marriage contract between the children of two lower lords, assigning an appropriate dowry price for the bride. However, it was the next case that caught her attention.

A young man was led into the room. He walked in slowly, bound in thick, silver chains which encircled both his wrists and ankles, forcing him to shuffle between them. The men on either side of him wore the black robes of the Periculum Guard. She studied the young man more closely as he was led closer to the marble steps. With sun-kissed skin and dark red hair, the boy could barely have been more than fifteen. His clothes were brown, the simple garment of a farmer or merchant of the lower class. She glanced to where Chiro stood, but he offered only a blank expression as the young boy was forced to his knees at the bottom of the stairs leading to the throne. Cases involving those of the lower classes were never brought before the throne. The appearance of this man was highly irregular.

She turned her attention to the men who had escorted the young man into the throne room. "Your Royal Highness," the guard on the right addressed her. "We have been sent on behalf of the High Lord of Periculum."

"I welcome the Guards of Periculum to the Royal Court," she addressed them with the expected formality. "Please, my lords, tell me what brings you before me today."

Again, the man on the right spoke. "My princess, this boy has been found guilty of murder."

Mary's eyes snapped to the man who spoke. "Murder?"

"Yes, my princess. And for his crime, this man, Cedrick Felton, has been sentenced to death."

"Death?" She looked at the boy kneeling before the throne. He was thin, scrawny, and looked absolutely miniature compared to the guards surrounding the princess. "Tell me what happened."

"My princess," he stated. "You need not concern yourself with the details as I assure you, the high lord was very through. Your uncle would always sign the orders as he saw fit."

Mary drew a deep breath and straightened in her silver chair. "Well, as you can see, my lords, I am not my uncle and I have no intention of signing a death warrant without knowing the particulars of the case." She shifted her gaze to the boy on the floor. "How old are you, Cedrick?"

Startled at being addressed, the boy looked up. "Fifteen, my lady."

"It's princess," the guard on his left interrupted. "Lady is a lower rank."

The boy's cheeks flushed, but Mary intervened. "It is fine," she stated. "I would not expect you to know the particulars of royal protocol. Not tell me what this is all about."

"My princess," the guardsman spoke again. "The boy is a known thief. He has been caught on several occasions, running around with a group of troublemakers about the same age. They have caused a great deal of problems over the past few years in their town. But, well, never resulting in more than theft until now."

Mary nodded. "Go on."

"There is a small village outside the Temple of Occidere which has been having some issues with raiders coming down from the Usqub Mountains. Members of the Usqub guard and a few others were sent to help defend the villagers." He motioned to the boy kneeling in the thick chains. "A member of the guard was walking the streets of the village, two young men walked behind them. The first tried to steal the guard's purse, cutting it from the guard's waist and attempting to run off with the gold coins inside. Realizing what was happening, the guard turned and grabbed the young man's arm, forcing it behind him and causing the gold to drop to the ground.

"When he did this, however, this man," he motioned again to the prisoner, "grabbed the guard's arm, pulling it off of his friend and effectively knocking him to the ground. The guard, he…"

"He hit his head," the man said. "The healer said he died instantly."

Mary stared down at the boy. Thin, malnourished, not even an adult by temple standards. She turned her gaze to Chiro seeking an explanation to her unspoken questions, but he remained silent, forcing her to ask the questions herself.

"Forgive me," she spoke to the two guardsmen. "It sounds like what you are describing is a tragic accident. One that should never have occurred, of course and should be punished within an appropriate level. But…" She shook her head. "Surely this is not to the level of an execution. In fact…forgive me, my lords, but I do not understand why this matter has been brought to me personally. It seems like an issue for the lower lords at the temples masters."

"It is, my princess. The temple masters who insisted the case be brought before you."

"Why?" she asked in confusion. "It was an accident. He's only a boy."

"Your Highness." The man on the right cleared his throat. "Forgive me, but, you see, the guardsman was not a member of the general Usqub Guard. It was Hayden Muercer."

"Muercer," Mary repeated, searching her memory. Why did she feel that she knew that name? "Muercer…"

It was Kyle, standing on the right side of her throne, who said, "Muercer, as in the lord and a former Temple Master of Bellum?"

"His son."

"The silver student of Bellum? He is dead?"

"Yes."

Kyle took a step to the edge of the marble steps, staring down at the boy on the floor. "By the Gods."

Mary's mind raced with a thousand thoughts flying too quickly for her to fully comprehend any of them. She had not known Hayden well, but had a vague memory of a younger man with short brown hair, garbed in the silver robes of one who had earned such a rank. He would have been a contender for the thirteenth tournament. Not enough to be a contender for the crown, but enough to possibly earn a place on the Defendant Team.

"The son of a former temple master," she said. "I…"

She was saved by Chiro who spoke from the left side of her chair where he had stood opposite his son. "My lords," he addressed the two men. "The princess shall take some time to review this matter in more detail and shall have an answer to your request shortly. I will have your prisoner escorted to the tower and you shall be given quarters within the palace grounds until this matter is resolved."

"I thank you, my lord; my princess," the guardsmen said as they turned to leave the room, leading their prisoner between them to the sound of clattering metal.

Chapter XLII

Mary sat in one of her private sitting rooms at a large desk of dark red wood. Before her sat a stack of papers which she had read so many times she could recite them from memory. She went again and again over the various incident reports collected. They all said the same thing. The boy pushed Hayden in an attempt to free his friend. The event should not have resulted in more than a few scrapes and bruises. Instead, a silver student of the temples was dead. She gave a frustrated sigh as the door opened and Chiro entered the room.

She looked up at the high lord. "I know what you are here for," she said. "I'm sorry. I do not have an answer."

Chiro walked closer to where she sat and pulled up a chair. "With your permission?"

"Please."

He seated himself beside her. "My princess," he began. "Ultimately this choice must be yours. You are, after all, the queen and the choice of life and death of such issues lies with you alone. However, you have appointed me head of your Royal Council and therefore, I would be remiss in my duties if I did not advise you now."

She offered a nod. "Okay, my lord. You have my attention."

"This is not going to be easy for you to hear, my lady. In fact, I am fairly certain it will be unwelcome."

"Have you reviewed these papers? There is nothing about this scenario that shows this as anything more than an accident."

"This is not your job, princess."

She shook her head. "I don't understand."

"It is the role of the high lords and temple masters to determine the facts of the events and the appropriate punishment for the crime. It is the role of the queen only to ensure that they did their job thoroughly and that the verdict is within the confines of the law of both the crown and the Gods."

"Chiro I think this was…"

"The facts are not in dispute. He killed Hayden Muercer. The son of a lord of the realm. A Royal Champion and a student of the temples whose students you are sworn to protect, both as acting queen and as the golden student of Kale. This man set out to commit an act which is against the law. The ultimate consequence may have been unintentional, but the act which lead to said results was purposefully committed." Chiro drew a deep breath. "This path became a possibility the moment he decided to break the laws of Kale."

"He is little more than a child. He is younger than I am."

"And yet, he still took a life."

"He was trying to protect his friend. From what these reports say, the boy barely pushed him. I mean," she shook her head, "would we even be here if it had been someone other than Hayden Muercer? Are we trying this boy for his crimes, or for the parentage of the man he, by these accounts, accidently killed?"

"My princess." He sighed. "I know that this is new to you. I know that the politics of the kingdom are something with which you were not raised nor trained to understand."

"Politics? Am I hearing you correctly? I am supposed to balance this boy's life - to decide on his death - because of politics?"

"Your Highness."

"No," she stated. "I am so sick and tired of all of these formality. We are alone in my private chambers discussing ending the life of a young, poor, sickly boy. I cannot take this right now. Please."

He stared at her for several moments before finally saying, "All right, Mariana. I know this is difficult for you to understand. But you asked me here, to be your voice and to help guide you through the inner working within the kingdom over which you now rule. I need you to listen to me now."

"I am."

"This young man was a silver student of a temple. You cannot allow his killer to go unpunished."

"Then we will put him in the tower," she said. "To kill him…that cannot be the answer."

"Actually," a second voice joined them as the golden doors opened and Master Jiro entered the room. "To lessen the punishment would be to publically declare that both the lords and masters involved in passing down the judgment as incompetent. It would cause those over whom they rule to question their judgments, both those made recently and those made previously."

Chiro nodded in acknowledgment of Jiro's words. "You would also be paying a grave insult to the Muercer family as well. They have paid great service to the realm. Both parents were defendants and Lord Muercer was a temple master. Hayden served as bravely as a silver student and gave his life protecting the realm. You must understand, Mariana, that the implications of your choice here tonight are far greater than the life of one man."

"He is barely more than a child. A child who made a horrible mistake, I grant you. But still…"

Jiro stepped closer to stand beside Chiro's chair. "Princess," he stated. "I am so sorry. But that is not your call or your job."

"But I am the queen!"

"Yes, my princess. And this, is a part of what that title means. It means making the hard choices. The choices that no one should ever be forced to make and yet, you are the only one who can."

The room suddenly seemed too hot. Mary stood from her chair, grabbing the stack of papers from the desk and thrusting them into Chiro's face. "This…you honestly think that this constitutes the need for an execution? The killing—the murder—of a fifteen-year-old, destitute, starving boy?"

"I do not believe that it is your decisions. The facts are not in dispute. The verdict is permissible under the laws of the temples, passed down from the Gods above. You, as queen of the Kalian bloodline, are bound to uphold those laws. You want the throne? This is a part of it. The worst part. But one you must learn to honor nevertheless."

Chiro stood from his chair and calmly placed the papers back onto the desk, smoothing them flat against the dark wood. From behind him, Jiro also moved and guided the princess back to her chair before taking a knee before her. "Mariana," he spoke firmly. "This is bigger than you and I. This young man who died, who this boy killed, is the son of a very powerful man. They are wealthy, ancient in their bloodline, loyal in their service to the realm, and important to the security of the kingdom and your throne. They have asked for the life of the man who murdered their son. It is a fair request, Mariana. I am sorry that this is hard for you, but…I am afraid there is no other way."

Chiro moved to stand behind the chair where Mary sat, placing his hand upon her shoulder. "Jiro is right, Mariana. This is what is right."

"I don't want to do this." But her voice was meek as she sat between the two powerful men.

Jiro reached forward and took her hands in his own as he continued to stare up into her eyes. "I am so sorry that this falls to you at such a young age. I know it is not what you wanted. I know it is not fair. However, you were born a princess and this..." She felt Chiro's fingers dig into both of her shoulders, guiding her to turn in the chair to better face the desk. "Mariana," Jiro stated. "This is for the good of the kingdom."

The temple master then transferred both of her delicate hands into the grasp of his left hand, while he reached toward the desk with his right as Chiro continued to press down lightly upon her shoulders. Then Jiro raised her hand to the desk and placed a quill into the palm of her right hand, slipping it carefully between her fingers before guiding her hand to the paper. "He murdered the son of a defendant and temple master," Jiro spoke again. "This is what you must do."

"Why?" she asked in a mere whisper.

"Consider this, Mariana. If this was Kyle, or any member of the temple in which you have personally served, would you have to ask this question?"

She squeezed her eyes shut, trying desperately to make sense of the turmoil in her mind. Instead, she saw Kyle lying on the floor, his life blood spilling from his pale skin. She remembered the warm wetness as it cascaded across her hands, and how she tried desperately to save him from death's inevitable grasp. *If it was Kyle.*

Mary opened her deep green eyes. Her signature stood clearly against the yellowed parchment beneath her hand.

Chapter XLIII

―――◆➣◆✵◆≾◆―――

Ameria clutched the silver blade, staring across the golden mats at Lord Stephen. The training room had been built centuries ago, but had been constantly kept in pristine condition by the high lords. The walls were lined with portraits of the lords who had fought and ruled in these sacred halls, dating back for centuries and with paint that had become more and more faded over the years. The Silver Defendant had served as her sparring partner during the previous weeks, ensuring that she maintained her training in preparation for the final tournament looming in the distance.

Ameria raised her sword, easily blocking Stephen's own as it came smashing down upon her own. She slid her blade along the side of his, the sound of screeching metal shattering the room. They had been sparing for a while. Their breathing became labored as they turned and twisted upon the golden mats. Ameria moved, bringing her sword up against Stephen's left side. He jumped to his right, avoiding the blade in the nick of time. The two continued to circle each other for several moments as she waited for her opponent's next move.

He lunged, bringing his blade down toward Ameria's right. She calmly moved her blade, bending her knees to better resist his superior weight, and blocking the movement, her hands clutching the hilt. She stepped back and then swept her sword right in an arc. Stephen moved to block, but was too slow and the tip of the blade reached his side. Yet, as it began to slice through the satin material of his silver robes, Ameria stopped the blade with perfect precision.

"You lose," she stated calmly, stepping back and placing her clean blade back securely in its sheath at her side.

She offered a low bow of respect and then turned to leave the room. She walked down a long series of corridors. She had spent the last few weeks with her grandfather, learning all she could about the old stories of the Gods and wraiths, and gathering the pieces of her parents' story. It had never been a love match, Ameria had always known that. However, the length of tactics taken to ensure the marriage of these two families was partially new information. Ameria had never considered herself to be much of a romantic, but the thought that her father had spent the better part of his life living with a woman who had literally been forced upon him made her wonder at the fate that awaited her, should she in deed defeat her sister and become the next queen. In all likelihood, Kyle would be the highest ranking of the men. But…what if he was not?

She considered the question for a while. Though her parents' marriage had been loveless, it had also been successful from a political standpoint. The idea of going to bed with a nameless stranger held a sense of discomfort, though it was far from the sheer horror she imagined her sister would face if Mary found herself being forced to consent to the same fate. Her sister's open acceptance of the Oath of Blood and Arms surprised her at first, but then after contemplation, she came to determine that the act was more likely a command given by Master Leo than one of her sister's own volition. She would consider it a strange twist of fate that Leo would die as nearly twenty years of scheming stood on the edge of falling into place.

Yet, over the past few weeks, Ameria had come to suspect that nothing in their recent lives was the result of fate, but instead of some grand design which she was not yet capable of understanding. She walked to the back of the ancient castle and stepped onto the balcony, which had become her favorite place at sunset. She stared out into the horizon with the last of the suns' rays shimmering against her golden robes.

Wraiths. Gods. Fate. Destiny. *Fear to the fearless. Hope to the hopeless. Mercy to those who hate you. Death to those who love you. Princess of Kale. Princess of Koloso. Heir to Both.* But…what did it mean? She attempted, as she did, most evenings, to make sense of words which always seemed to lie just beyond her grasp. "What does it mean?" she asked softly, the gentle wind swirling her words around her before vanishing into the encroaching shadows. "Please," she said again. "I want to understand."

The wind continued to spiral around her, blowing her robes behind her and pushing back the long locks of her golden hair. She nearly jumped out of her skin when a deep, rough voice spoke.

"Princess of Kale."

Her heart lurched in her throat and she momentarily forgot to draw breath.

"Princess of Koloso."

She turned as though in slow motion. There, standing upon all four paws, was the wraith. Its black fur rustled in the breath of the cool wind. Its slanted, catlike eyes reflected the light of the dying suns. Its deadly white teeth slid forth from the corners of its mouth surrounded by lips of an unnatural crimson. Ameria stared at the wraith trapped between terror and a fierce desire to know why it had appeared. *With the vengeance of the Gods*, her grandfather's words echoed through the back of her mind.

She forced herself to the ground, entering the position of a traditional Kalian bow before the messenger of the Gods. She swept her hair to one side, exposing her pale neck to the wraith, a sign of required respect and surrender to the highest of all great powers. Her voice arose steady, despite the racing of her heart. "My lord."

She felt the eyes of the wraith studying her, and it took a step closer. "Princess of the most ancient and royal of all bloodlines," he stated in a deep, gruff voice. "I have come to answer your prayer."

She forced herself to draw a tight, yet steady breath. "I am at your service, oh God of Kale."

"I am no God," the wraith replied, moving close enough that she could feel its warm breath on the back of her skin. "Only a servant. As are you."

She forced herself to raise her head enough to stare into the wraith's eyes. They were not a particular color, but a sparkling spectacle of reflective light, always glinting and never steady. "I am ready to serve, my lord. Please, tell me what the Gods require. I shall give it willingly."

He stared directly into her gaze. "Calmness through fear. Precision in every act. Graceful and powerful. Rage controlled with such clarity. Beautiful yet deadly. A true child of the Kalian bloodline. Many have come before you. Yet none with your depth of soul, emotional yet controlled. Yes, you will do well in what the Gods have in store for you, Princess of Kale."

"You have watched over us from childhood."

"Yes," the wraith hissed. "We protect the twins of the ancient bloodline until the time comes for them to fulfill their destiny. The time draws near now. Yes. The time draws close indeed."

A chill crawled along her spine. "What would you have of me, my lord? I am ready to serve the Gods."

"Not yet, my princess. So close and yet, you still cannot see."

"Then please, my lord, guide me."

"Tell me this, daughter of Kale. Daughter of Koloso. Would you seek vengeance upon those who stole your father's life?"

She straightened, but did not dare to rise from her kneeling position. "I desire nothing more."

"Then I am here to fulfill your desire, princess. I shall guide you to your father's killer. But know this, daughter of Kale. Once you begin this path, there will be no turning back."

Ameria gave a hard swallow as she continued to stare into the inhuman eyes of the wraith and spoke without hesitation. "I am ready, my lord. I have been ready since the prince drew his last breath."

The wraith gave a rough laugh. "You are indeed the daughter of Kale. Now rise up and solve the mystery. You are so close." The vision of the wraith standing before her began to fade to shadow. It shivered in the evening air and then moved upon a gust of wind toward the tall door of the ancient castle of Serenitas. "Rise, princess," the shadow whispered, hovering in the air before the large stone door.

She stood in a graceful movement and walked briskly towards the shimmering darkness. It lead her through the hallways of the palace, twisting and turning down corridor after corridor until she eventually came to the door of the room where she had been staying. She entered the room to find it exactly as she had left it earlier that morning. "What? I don't understand."

"Come, princess," the shadow whispered, moving toward the large desk on the far wall. Ameria stepped forward, standing before the large mirror, unable to see her reflection through the formless shadow which lay in a thick sheet over the glass. "See, princes. Can you see?"

She moved closer. The desk appeared as it had been left that morning. The golden trophies clustered on the narrow plank. She studied the mirror but could not see through it. Then the shadow reached, sliding around her left wrist. It was cold to the touch, nearly freezing, and her arm jerked back involuntarily. As though a rope, the shadow encircled and tightened against her scarred wrist so sharply she almost cried out. "See, princess! See!"

She gazed into the mirror, but still could see nothing through the overlay of the shadowy figure. Then her gaze trailed down to the desk upon which the golden trophies sat. The shadowed rope guided her hand to one of the trophies which sat in the center of the desk before releasing its icy grasp on her hand. Far more shaken than when the wraith had been in physical form, she wrapped her fingers around the indicated trophy and picked up the award. *Tournament of Koloso Royal Championship* stood clearly etched into the gold, but as she had noted several weeks before, the name of the champions were missing. She ran her hand over the engraving and found it completely smooth to the touch, as though the name had never existed.

"Never existed," the shadow whispered her thoughts.

She pulled it closer and again ran her finger over the missing name. *No, not as though it had never existed. As though it had been removed. Smoothed away and replaced with an additional layer of gold, so that not even the scratch marks would remain.*

"What?" she said aloud, then moved the trophy to her left side and reached for the next: *Tournament of Kale Royal Championship: Lady Annabelle Berhea & Lord Jiro Darian of Koloso.* She picked up another. *Tournament of Critous Royal Championship: Lady Annabelle Berhea & Lord Jiro Darian of Koloso. Tournament of Deasto, Proelum, Saltatio. Of Koloso.* "Wait," she spoke as though the shadow was unaware of her every thought. "Of Koloso?"

She picked up the trophy with the missing name and again read the inscription. *Tournament of Koloso Royal Championship.* There were two.

"Andrew's?" Though no sooner did the though enter her mind, she realized that it was an impossibility. Her mother and uncle had fought in the same year. There was only one Royal Championship awarded. She turned and started counting the trophies. She continued to sort through them and found an additional replica, this one from the Temple of Kale. She gazed up at the shadow as the world began to shift. "If these are my mother's," a feeling of dread beginning to overcome her, "then whose trophies are these?"

The shadow lowered itself from the mirror and stopped several feet in front of where she knelt between the golden trophies, and again began to take physical form. When the wraith was solid enough, it leaned towards her. "No going back, Daughter of Kale. Daughter of Koloso."

Ameria wanted to pause, to think, but she knew any such action would result in the truth escaping her forever. "Show me."

With those words, the wraith leaned closer, bringing its teeth perilously close to her scarred hands, which clutched the nameless Kolosian trophy. He blew his searing breath across the golden surface, and as she watched, letters began to burn themselves into the gold. The name covered over long ago appeared upon the metal in heated light. Ameria had to blink against the light and fought against the urge to release her hold on the burning metal. Yet she forced herself to keep the trophy within her grasp, as she gazed down to read the name now etched upon its previously smooth surface. *Tournament of Koloso Royal Championship: Lady Angelia Berhea & Lord Nathaniel Crestal of Koloso.* She turned to gaze into the shadow, but instead found herself staring into her grandfather's jade green eyes.

Chapter XLIV

THE HIGH LORD OF SERENITAS stood tall in his crisp golden robes, leaning on the matching handle of his otherwise dark cane. He stared at Ameria in silence from the doorway, but the look was enough to know that he had seen what had transpired. She rose from the floor to face him.

"All my life," her grandfather spoke in a reserved tone. "I have waited all my life. All my life I have prayed and served. And yet it is only now, at the end that they have come." Ameria remained still, glancing at her grandfather with a tense silence. "They have come for the twins of Kale."

Ameria glanced down at the trophy in her hands and held it towards her grandfather. He stepped forward, his cane striking the dark stone as he moved to take the trophy from her hands. "Who is she, Grandfather? And why was she fighting with the father of the man responsible for killing my father and the Master of the Kalian Temples."

Lord Riccard drew a deep breath and began to walk down the hall. "Follow me, princess. I will show you."

She followed him without question, walking down the long hallways until they came before a large door which Ameria had never entered. Riccard reached into his inner robes and withdrew a ring of small keys, one of which he inserted into the lock, and pushed the door open with a loud series of creaks. He motioned her into the room and then followed her inside. Even in the dim light, she could see the thick layers of dust which covered the furniture, enveloping the small desk on the right side of the door. Inside, much as in her mother's room, everything was gold, though the former brilliance of the satin material covering the bed and sofa had long ago faded. Ameria gazed around the room for several moments before she walked towards a shelf on the far side upon which stood a set of additional trophies. Like the others, the names had been removed. However, as she reached, her hand touching the trophy on the farthest edge of the desk, the names bled through, the same two names appearing on each one. Temple of Saltatio, Bellum, Critous, Kevera, Dektra, Desoto,

Postrema, Proelium, Eight in total sat upon the shelf. Combined with those of the Temple of Kale and Koloso, that meant they had won ten of the twelve Temple Tournaments, and all those held in the highest ranking of the temples.

"Ten wins," Ameria said. "Ten wins. That is…"

"As many as your mother won, yes."

"But…" She turned staring around the room encased in gold. She walked towards the bed and looked at the dust-covered blankets. The mark of Koloso was etched into the fabric, covering the bed. "I don't understand," she finally said, turning back to her grandfather who had followed her a few paces into the room.

"I suppose it was only a matter of time until you learned the truth. If your father had been killed by another, the secret may have remained buried. When your mother informed me of who was responsible for your father's death, I insisted that you be told at once. However, she bound me to the oath we made long ago. An oath which now, by the grace of the Gods, I am now required to break."

"What are you talking about?" She turned more fully towards him. "What is going on? Who is Angelia?"

His gaze hardened as he began to answer. "Lady Angelia Esmeralda Berhea was a Lady of Serenitas, former Golden Student of Koloso and younger sister to Princess Annabelle Dektra, your mother."

"My mother's sister?" she asked in confusion. "You mean, your daughter? You have another daughter?"

"Had another daughter."

"Had? I don't…why would you wipe her name from the trophies? Why have I never heard of her before?"

"Because she was named a traitor and banished from the kingdom."

"A traitor?" Her mind searched through the swirl of information she had been desperately collecting since first riding to her grandfather's door. The king had married without the approval of the temples. Her mother and Master Leo had assisted in the fight against the armies of Agnus. Her father's real love had died, clearing the way for Annabelle to be married to the Crown Prince. She racked her brain, but no mention of Angelia came to her mind. "I have an aunt. A child of Serenitas…your child. Who was banished? I don't…" She shook her head. "Did she assist Nathaniel in killing the woman my father loved?"

"No." The word was sharp as the high lord confessed his family's shame. "But she chose to be exiled, nevertheless."

"Chose?"

Lord Riccard nodded. "Nathanial was the son of the High Lord of Flos. It was a good match for a second born daughter. My son would inherit the Province of Serenitas. Angelia and her children, the Province of Flos, and your mother, the throne. Our family would have been secured in their rightful place as the most powerful in the land, a level of safety at last from the threat of the High Lord of Turbamentum. But somewhere in my plans, I made a mistake. Your aunt fell in love with the young lord and when his punishment was handed down, she declared that she would join him in the exile of the Periculum Mountains."

He looked at her. "My daughter was foolish and fool-hearted. I informed her that if she left with Lord Nathaniel that she would be banished forever. That both she and any potential children would be denied their birthright. She vanished in the night. I sent men after her, but it was to no avail. She had disappeared." Her grandfather drew a deep breath and then motioned to the opposite side of the bed. "She left the note, which lies on the pillow exactly where I found it."

Ameria walked back to the bed. There, tucked between the golden pillows lay the small envelope with her grandfather's name written in delicate handwriting. She opened the letter carefully, the paper yellowed after years of exposure to the cool air of the bedroom.

My Dearest Father,

I am sorry to leave you so abruptly and that it has, at last, come to this. I know that you do not want to believe me, but Nathan is innocent of the crimes of which he has been accused. He never would have harmed another defendant of his own volition. I know that the Golden Defendant has rules on this matter, and that his word is law. However, his determination is wrong. I know that Nathan did not harm Lilian, I know it in my heart and in my soul. Lord Leo is wrong. Nathan is being punished for circumstances which were beyond his control and this is a grave injustice by which I cannot abide.

Please do not blame Nathan for this decision, for it is one I have made on my own accord. In fact, Nathan has begged me to stay with you - to not allow this horror to ruin my life as well as his own. However, I am determined, now more than ever, that if he is to face the loneliness of exile, it is one I am prepared to endure by his side. I have sworn to love stand beside him no matter what the cost, good or bad. This is not a vow I can break—even for you, whom I care for more deeply than any master I have ever served. I pray that you will find it in your heart to one day forgiven this transgression. Please know that I leave not out of spite or disobedience—but out of love. I love him, Father, and I cannot bear to live this life without him, even if it means I must live without ever seeing you again.

Please, if you can find it in your heart, tell my sister that I am sorry as well. I never meant for this to happen but I must follow my consciousness. You have always taught me to follow my heart, Father. This is the path I must now take.
Your eternally loving daughter,
Angelia Esmerelda Berhea

Ameria looked up and carefully refolded the letter, placing it back upon the pillow before turning to her grandfather and leveling her gaze to meet his own. "So what you are saying, Grandfather, is that your daughter, my aunt, fled with a traitor. A traitor." Her mind slid to the horrifying truth. "A daughter who gave birth to three sons."

Riccard stared at her for a long time and finally nodded. "Yes. Three sons whose crimes would shame this noble house forever—should the truth of their identities be revealed."

"Her sons killed my father. Their uncle."

The air seemed even colder as she walked across the room to reach her grandfather's side. She stared at him, her sapphire eyes gazing directly into his deep green ones. "You know that this will not stop me from killing them."

He returned her gaze. "Yes. They have killed the Gods chosen. They must die for their crimes."

"And the line of Serenitas? Will it die with them?"

"No, Ameria Dektra. It will continue…with you."

"With me?"

"Yes. I am prepared to declare you heir to all I have. And your children thereafter."

"Your heir?"

"Yes, my granddaughter."

"But Andrew…"

"Is unfit to rule." He continued to hold her gaze. "I declare my loyalty, and the loyalty of all of Serenitas, to you - Princess Ameria of Koloso."

"I…I don't..."

"Should you become queen, then your second born child shall inherit this land. Should you instead become the Golden Defendant, then you shall inherit all that this land has to offer. You are the heir I was denied the day my daughter chose to go into exile. You are the child of my mind, and of a matching soul to my own. I offer you my loyalty, Princess of Koloso. To you, and no other."

Chapter XLV

─◆•═⊃•✵•⊂═•◆─

MARY STOOD SILENTLY AS SHE watched the verdict carried out. Kyle and Chiro had both attempted to convince her that she did not have to be present for the actual execution, but she had simply turned to them and asked, "How can I be expected to sign this order, if I cannot even watch the order carried out?"

The question had ended the conversation, placing Mary in her current position of sitting astride her golden stallion several yards away as the boy was led from the highest tower and over the bright blue grass. A platform of gray stone stood on the side of the palace tower, built specifically for such an occasion. She dismounted from the horse and walked to the gray stone. Lord Chiro had unrolled a piece of parchment to pronounce the sentence, but stopped at the approach of the princess. She climbed the cracked steps to where the boy was being held between the two men and walked to Chiro's side, taking the parchment from his fingers.

"My princess," he whispered. "You do not have to do this."

She lowered her head, half closing her eyes as she smoothed the edges of the paper in her hands. "If I am to be queen, then I must do what is required of me."

"This is not among your duties, my lady."

"Yes," she corrected. "I believe it is." Chiro considered her for several moments before bowing his head and moving several paces to her right. She drew in a deep breath and turned to face the small crowd of guardsmen and a few members of both the victim's and the accused's family. She continued to smooth the paper in a nervous gesture. The faded, hollow tone with which she addressed them matched the dull ache in her chest and she could not help glancing again at the boy whose life had fallen so cruelly into her hands.

She had gone over the order so many times over the last two days that she did not need to look down to know what it said, yet she raised the paper anyway. It was not a long proclamation but merely the simplest of statements for the gravest of occasions. "Cedrick Felton of the Province of Periculum. You have been found guilty of the murder of the son of your rightful lord. For this crime, I, Crown Princess and acting queen of the Kalian bloodline, in concurrence with the High of Periculum, hereby hand out the sentence of death." She forced herself to draw the breath required to continue. "May the Gods grant you forgiveness with your death." Then she turned and forced herself to meet his terrified gaze.

He rushed and knelt at her feet, grabbing the edge of her golden robes. "Please, princess. Please don't let them do this," he begged. "I don't want to die."

Chiro jerked Mary back, forcing her away from the pleading child, for that is how he appeared—a scared, frightened child. The palace guard jerked him to his feet. "No!" he screamed. "I don't want to die. Don't do this!" Mary felt tears threatening her eyes as Chiro guided her farther back from the screaming prisoner. Her body began to shake as she watched him dragged to a raised block, his neck arched over the gray stone. "Don't kill me!" he begged even as they held him down. "Help me, please help me."

Chiro attempted to turn Mary away, but she fought his hands. She resisted the urge to shout out, to order this to stop. It was there, within her power. The child was shaking, crying, begging. Mary's heart was in her throat and suddenly, she knew this was an act she would not be willing to live with. She parted her lips as the blade came down. It slid through the skin of his neck biting deeply into the veins and arteries below. Blood spewed forth as the body jerked and convulsed at the sudden contact. She stared down at the body, watching the blood spread across the gray stone.

Marcus' voice rose on the hollow wind. *You killed me, Mary.*

It was only then that Mary turned, using the last of her strength to keep her tears from falling as she turned towards Chiro. "It's done."

"My lady, I am..." He shook his head. "I am sorry my lady, but this had to be done. It was the only way."

She did not answer him, but instead turned numbly and walked back to her golden stallion. She mounted the horse and turned back towards the palace. Kyle, who had never dismounted, turned along with her, following in silence upon his silver steed. They rode through the wide field, the wind holding a deep chill in the evening air.

It was your choice. The words seemed to nip at her heels as she urged her horse to a faster pace. It took several minutes to reach the palace, where she dismounted in a single stride, tossing Sherwyn's reins to one of the men guarding the door.

Kyle dismounted only moments behind her as she began to race down the hall back towards her private chambers. "Princess," he called.

"Not now."

"My lady."

"No."

When she finally reached her room, she closed the golden door. It did not matter though, as it opened moments later with Kyle following her.

"Go away!"

"I can't do that."

"It wasn't a request!"

"Please, listen to me."

"I did what you wanted!" She found herself screaming. "What more do you want from me? What more could you possibly want from me?"

"Nothing, my lady," came his surprisingly calm response. "Only to be here when you need me."

She looked at him, her anger beginning to slip from her grasp. *You killed me, Mary.* She walked forward, closing the distance between them. Her screams faded to whispers as she said, "Help me."

He reached to caress the side of her face, pushing back the strands of her long dark hair. "What would you have of me, my lady?"

She gazed into his jade green eyes so similar to her own. "Help me," she whispered again.

"Anything within my power to give." He repeated the promise he had made her so long ago.

"Please, Kyle. Please. I…I don't want this. I don't want any of this. I don't want to be a queen. I don't want to rule. I don't want this! I…I just…"

"Just what?"

The words escaped before she could stop them. "I want you." She drew a ragged breath. "I just want you."

His eyes searched hers and he pulled her closer, sliding his hand to the back of her neck. "Mariana," he whispered, his fingers tracing along the edge of her skin.

Her eyes closed at his gentle touch. "Please," she whispered.

Kyle's lips descended upon hers. Yet no sooner did they touch, Marcus' voice crept into the room. *Murderer*, it whispered. *You killed me, Mary. He killed Jace. What a perfect match you make—killers, murderers; death to those who love you!*

She jerked back as though burned.

Murder, death…a choice.

"Stop it," she spoke to the wordless voice.

"My lady?" Kyle asked in confusion.

A choice…

"Stop it. Stop it!"

You killed me, Mary. You killed me.

"No!" She was all but shrieking, raising her hands to cover her ears in a futile attempt to block out the voice which existed only in the confines of her mind.

Your choice.

She lowered her hands and raked her nails down both of her arms deep enough to draw blood, desperate for anything that would allow her to escape the torment.

"My lady, don't!" Kyle grabbed both her arms, forcing them away from her body. "Damn it, Mary: look at me!" Kyle demanded. "Look at me!"

She forced herself to focus on the sound of his voice. She opened her eyes to meet his gaze. Her words dimmed to a whisper. "Help me."

"How, my lady?"

She drew a series of short, unsteady breaths. "Make it stop, Kyle. Please." She leaned and buried her face against his chest. "Please, make it stop."

Kyle slid his arms around her, pulling her close, moving his hand to run gently through the long strands of her dark hair. "Mary," he murmured softly. "Mary, Mary, Mary."

She clung to him like the scared child she had never been. She felt small enfolded against him, safe between the strong arms which held her close. When her breathing finally began to steady, she did not pull away, but instead spoke in a haunted voice: "Yes."

It was only after she had spoken that she realized the meaning; the answer to the repeated question. "It was my choice."

"What?" he asked. "What is it, my lady?"

"It was my choice," she said again. "I chose you. It could have been anyone—not only Marcus, but anyone I had ever known, anyone I had ever loved—and still, I chose you." She placed her hands on opposite sides of Kyle's face, her dark eyes searching his. "I chose you," she repeated, "and, Gods help me, I would do so again." She leaned forward and kissed him. Then pulled back, her fears chased away by a horrible moment of clarity.

She would have chosen Kyle over Marcus. This stranger—this rival—for the life of a man who had fought by her side for over a decade. Her best friend, her most trusted companion, her partner, and she had given his life away without pause for the life of a rival. And she would do so again.

The truth stole her breath. The depth of her love was defined by the horrifying lengths she had gone to in order to ensure it would continue. It was a truth which should have sent her reeling; should have forced her into a dark pit of guilt and self-loathing so deep she would never again see the light of day. Yet, staring into Kyle's emerald eyes, she knew—it would not.

She stepped closer and again met his lips with a deep, searing kiss, pouring all of her anger, her passion, her pain into the kiss until it washed away all feelings except for one—desire. With her lips molded to his, Mary moved her hands down the back of his shirt, pausing just above his waist. She dug her fingers into the silver cloth, jerking on the satin material, pulling it from the security of his tightly cinched belt.

"My lady," he began.

She jerked up on the shirt, standing on her toes in order to lift the material over his broad shoulders. It fell to the floor moments later, revealing the panels of his smooth chest. His dark hair fell straight when the shirt was lifted, fully exposing the set of long jagged scars running down his face and neck—twin scars forever marking the sisters' deadly precision.

She softly kissed the edge of the scar on his neck, placed there by her sister's blade.

He shivered at her touch. "My lady, I..." She silenced him with another kiss. But as she pulled back he spoke again, this time addressing her by the dreaded title: "Princess."

"Don't!" She pressed herself closer so that her lips touched his skin as she spoke. "Please, don't."

He stood frozen at her touch, afraid to breathe as her hot breath warmed his skin against the cool night air. "Please," she asked again, planting a soft kiss upon his chest between each word. "Please, Kyle. I am asking, begging..."

Another shudder raced through him at the sound of her voice, his arms slipping around her at her desperate need. His right hand finally cupped the side of her face, lifting her gaze to meet his own. He could see the unshed tears in her eyes.

She drew a shivering breath and finally asked, "Tell me that you do not love me."

He pressed his lips to hers, silencing the unwanted question, his other arm slipping around her shoulders. He kissed her thoroughly, holding her tightly against him. She attempted to place her arms around him, but Kyle dug his fingers deeply into her left shoulder, forcing her arm to stay at her side. Then, he pulled back.

"My lady," he stated in a calm voice that did not match the passion which had been conveyed in the kiss. He took her hand and guided her to the opposite side of the room before seating her upon the golden coverlet of the bed. He then lowered himself down to one knee before her, so that he was forced to gaze up at her from the position. "My lady."

The edges of her heart began to crumble at the repeated formal address. "Kyle, I don't..."

"I love you," he said. "Enough to pledge my heart, my soul and my honor. But..." His words began to fail and he found himself forced to draw a deep breath in order to continue. "You are a princess—my princess. Nothing can change this - even love."

"Then don't refuse me," she begged through trembling lips. "Don't leave me to some faceless champion chosen by nothing more than a cruel twist of fate." She could not keep the tears from her voice. "If you love me. If you..."

"I do love you, Mary," Kyle found himself struggling not to rise up and crush her in his arms, his calm demeanor a barely hidden mask that was beginning to crack under the weight of her pain. He forced himself to meet her wild gaze. "Tell me," he finally said, "that the Gods are false. That the oath you swore means nothing, and I will take you in my arms right here, right now. Say the words, Mariana." He drew a long breath. "Say the words."

She stared down at the man kneeling before her, willing to lay everything, his very honor, at her feet. "Kyle." His name escaped her lips as a broken sob. "I...I... Princess. Queen. Undefeated Kalian Champion. What good is any of it, if we... If I..."

A violent tremor danced along her spine. Kyle reached for her, instinctively taking her hands in his own, wanting nothing more than to wipe the pain from her eyes. "Mary...you have to say the words."

She continued to stare down willing the lie to form upon her lips when her gaze rose involuntary from her would-be lover's eyes to the tall, glass window with the dark curtains blowing in the stormy winds.

The wraith stared back, his cat-like eyes reflective even in the dim light. Her heart began to pound as the eyes held her in silent warning. *Remember*, the voiceless words slid across the room, *a consequence to every choice, Princess of Kale*. Her heart jumped to her throat, her body going completely still under its dark gaze. *Your choice, princess. Your choice*. Then he was gone.

She turned her gaze back to Kyle's, biting her lip in an effort to keep her tears from falling. "No," she finally whispered. "I will not take the honor of the man who has sworn his life to protect my own." For several moments Kyle stared up at her, attempting to comprehend the sudden fear he saw shining through her emerald eyes. He then stood from his kneeling position and turned to gather his shirt when she said, "Wait."

He turned instantly back to face her.

"Kyle, can you…"

"What would you have of me, my lady?"

"Would you stay here while I sleep?" she finally asked. She sounded young, fearful, nothing like the woman who had begged to be in his arms only moments before. "You can send in someone else, but I…"

He crossed the room in three quick strides. "I will stay, my lady."

She gave a slight nod and then turned away from him, pulling back the golden blankets to slip between the warmth they provided. He stepped quietly across the room and replaced his silver shirt, before taking his place against the far wall of the queen's bedchamber.

However, no sooner had her breathing stilled than she awoke screaming. She scrambled against the sheets, fighting their hold, half falling from the bed as he rushed to her side. "My lady."

"No!" she shrieked from the remnants of the nightmare. "No!"

"Mary!" he tried again, lifting her in his arms before sliding her back toward the center of the bed. "Mary." He wrapped his arms around her, her body shivering as a sound escaped her lips somewhere between a moan and a sob.

"I'm sorry. I'm sorry, I'm…"

"Shh," he quieted her. "It's okay."

Her body trembled violently as he drew her further into his arms. "You don't have to," she spoke through chattering teeth. "You can…"

"I'm not going anywhere." Her shaking grew worse as Kyle tightened his grip around her. "Mary, you're safe. I promise. I promise you are safe. I'm here. I'm here."

"Don't leave me." Her words betrayed her. "Please, Kyle. Don't leave me." It was only then that the first tear fell from her eyes, slipping down her cheek to fall on the silver satin of Kyle's shirt.

"I won't," he promised. "I won't leave you, Mary."

She sat in the circle of his arms for a long time before she found the strength to draw a deep breath. She lay back down upon the bed, pulling him with her. He held her close, allowing her body to lean against his chest. Neither spoke, but instead lay silently as he continued to hold her in his arms.

When sleep once again claimed her still form, Kyle raised his hand to the side of her face, brushing several strands of her dark hair away from her cheek. "What do you dream, my lady?" he whispered to the dark chambers, unaware of the watching eyes which held the answer he sought.

Chapter XLVI

4 Months Ago

Far north of the royal palace, Lady Angelia Berhea Crestal stared lividly at her eldest son. "And you left him there! In the hands of the women whose father you murdered!"

"Peter was dying," Alec replied heatedly. "What was I supposed to do?"

"You were not supposed to go after members of the royal family in the first place! Oh my Gods! Do you know what you have done?"

"Of course I do," he replied. "I avenged our father. I killed the men who wronged him!"

"Alec." Angelia's stomach reeled at the realization of what her son had done. "How could you?"

"I think I should be asking you the same question, Mother. How could you?"

Angelia took a step back. "What is that supposed to mean?"

"The girl that Ryan rescued. The one whose ankle you tended after her attack in the woods. She was the *Sutis* Princess of Kale! And you let Ryan walk her out of here!"

"I did not…"

"Do not bother to deny it, Mother. You knew she was the princess and yet you allowed her to leave anyway. The Princess of Kale in our clutches and you let her go. Father would never have been so weak."

"Your father would never have dishonored himself as you have. He accepted the verdict of the Golden Defendant with honor and dignity, and I stood by him. But you… You killed Prince Eadmund! By the Gods, you killed the prince of the realm."

Her son looked at her with a stranger's eyes. "Why don't you say it?"

"Say what?"

"What you actually mean, Mother. For once, just say it—out loud."

"You left your brother in the hands of a madman," she stated. "Your youngest brother!"

"Ryan could have left with us. He made his choice."

"The king of this realm is not going to care that it was you and not your brother who killed the Prince."

"Ah, but haven't you heard? The king died of his illness. Mariana, the princess who you had literally in our grasp, is now seated upon the throne." Alec took a step closer to her. "However, that is not what you wanted to say, is it, Mother?"

She eyed her son for several long moments. "I do not understand what you are asking, my son."

"But of course you do. Say it; out loud. And let the lies, at last, end here."

Angelia finally felt herself fighting down tears as the words slipped from her lips. "You killed your uncle."

He stared at her with a cruel expression. "And tell me, Mother, will you now, at last, turn from your children? Do you think that your father would take you back now?"

"No." She inhaled deeply. "But he is going to kill you. What you have done is an insult to the family honor, something which my father, the High Lord of Serenitas and now, grandfather to the Queen of Kale, will never allow to see the light of day. He will come for you with the wrath of the temples and all the power of his kingdom before allowing the princesses the personal honor of severing your head from your body." She shook her head. "You have no idea the wrath you have brought down upon us."

"And you, Mother. What will you do? Will you stand aside and watch as your children are murdered in front of you?"

Her gaze darkened as she stared at her eldest son. "You know that I cannot do that. But then again, you knew what I would do long before you forced me into this choice."

With those words, Angelia turned and left the room in a blind fury. She stormed down the halls, closing herself in her private chambers before lying down upon the bed. The room was simple, nothing compared to the grandeur of the world into which she had been born. Yet, together she and Nathan had managed to make a life and celebrate the life of their three beautiful children. But even in her happiest moments, she lived with a deep ache of regret for the family she had turned away from. How she had wished her father could have met his first grandchild, could have watched him grow. She envisioned the pride he would have had in teaching his grandsons the ways of the sword and the ancient traditions that he held so dear.

"May the Gods forgive me," she whispered. "How could my son have done such a thing?" She leaned across to the opposite side of the bed and wrapped her hand around a small portrait of Nathan. It was one of the few pictures she possessed of her husband, save for those in her memory. "Oh Nathan," she whispered to the husband who had died nearly fourteen years before of a severe illness. She had considered at the time, going back to her father. Begging him for mercy, not for herself, but instead for her children. Yet by then, it had been too late. Her name had been removed from the history books, her portraits removed from the family halls and the young princesses were being raised to believe that she had never even existed. A few years ago, she had taken a rare chance, donning her old temple robes and had managed to enter the Temple of Critous to watch their annual tournament where one of her nieces, Ameria, had won the day. Despite the long golden locks, there was no denying that she was, indeed, Annabelle's daughter. She fought with the same sharp precision, the same controlled tactic which had made her sister so fierce in the tournaments which eventually saw her crowned as a Princess of Kale.

While she was there, hidden among the crowds, she caught sight of the royal box and felt her breath catch as she saw her father seated among the other high lords. His dark hair had turned silver and his hand rested upon the golden handle of a long cane. But his stature was still tall, his features distinct with sharp cheek bones and piercing eyes. She could not help but watch him as the fights continued, the bored expression as he made occasional conversation with others sharing the box with him.

Then Princess Ameria stepped onto the golden mats. His eyes flew to the fight, all of his attention focused upon the golden-haired woman staring calmly at her equally ranked opponent. She dismissed those from the lower temples along with her silver-clad partner. One look was all that was required to determine that he could be none other than the son of Lord Chiro. Angelia watched the match, enamored with the grace and synchronization of the two partners twisting and turning along the golden mats as they defeated their opponents one by one, until they eventually emerged victorious. She felt a sense of pride watching her niece defeat her opponents so effortlessly. Yet it was the look on her father's face that caught her attention even more than Ameria's flawless efforts in the ring.

Her cold, aloof father's stern face was filled with pride. A smile split his normally grim features as he watched his granddaughter take a bow before the screaming crowd. It was a rare look, one that he had once reserved only for her. It made something deep inside her hurt knowing that it was a look she would never see given to her own children, who she had chosen to raise in the exile of the temples.

Her sister had come to her once not long after Alec's fifth birthday. "I don't care what Father said to you," Annabelle had stated. "I cannot change your husband's fate, nor the path you have chosen to follow. However, your children do not have to pay the price for what happened. The Temple of Desoto has agreed to take him on as a red student, with the opportunity for advancement as soon as he is ready. Lord Chiro has also agreed to say that he is a cousin of the Turbamentum family and will act as guardian, if one should be needed. He can be trained in the temple and perhaps even one day restored to his birthright as a Lord of Serenitas. At minimum he will have a chance to be a defendant."

Angelia had literally laughed in her sister's face. "You honestly think I would send my child back into the world of the temples?" she had demanded. "Under the power of the temple master who banished his father for a crime he never committed? To serve a king unworthy to rule a lower province, let alone the kingdom, and a prince whose rage allowed him to sentence an innocent man and your own sister into exile?" She began to laugh and it was a harsh, cruel sound. "You must be joking."

"You chose your exile," Annabelle reprimanded her. "You could have stayed! Father would have married you to Chiro and your children would be fit to inherit and rule both provinces! You chose to leave with Nathan and broke our father's heart in doing so."

"His heart, really? Like he ever had one."

Annabelle stared at her sister with a look that was raw, her normally schooled features expressive and vulnerable. "Only for you, dear sister. Only for you."

That had been the last time she had spoken to Annabelle and the regret of her words now ate at the deepest recesses of her soul. She had been angry that Leo had not relented when she had chosen to leave with Nathan. A part of her had believed that faced with the exile of the daughter of the highest Lord in the land, Nathan's transgressions might have been forgiven—at least enough to live out the rest of his days within the kingdom. She had been bitter as well, at the sister whose children would bear a royal title, while hers would never be acknowledged by the family she had chosen to forsake.

Love and power, her father would always say. *The two can never exist in the same world.* And yet, she knew that her father had loved her. Had watched her fight with proud eyes. Had given her, and not her sister, the necklace that he had once given to her mother. It was almost as though he had been allowed to love her, since he already had two heirs to groom in the ways of ruling. It was the only thing her sister had ever envied.

Yet now her son had declared war upon the princesses. He had developed a deep-seeded hatred for the family he should have been taught to love. This was her fault. She should have sent them to the temples. Should have sent them to the family who had offered to claim them, in spite of their parents' transgressions. "Oh Nathan," she whispered to the portrait clutched tightly in her hand. "What have we done?" She lay there a long time before finally rising slowly from the bed and walking towards the training room of the village temple.

The room was old and in disrepair. The curtains draping the cracked mats were faded and tattered. Yet, it had still served its purpose for the training of her three sons which first Nathan and then Angelia herself had commenced over the years. She walked past the squared off mats under the domed ceiling of the temple until she reached the back of the room. Once there, she closed her eyes, sliding her hand across the wall's rough surface until she found the small latch hidden against a corner shelf. She touched the latch, but still had to push with all her strength in order to opened the hidden door and enter the small room beyond.

It was covered in a thick layer of dust, almost completely empty save for a single chest sitting in the left corner of the room. After closing the door behind her, it was to this chest that Angelia walked. Kneeling down beside the ancient chest, Angelia blew a layer of dust from its surface, coughing as she raised the lid with a loud creak. Inside, wrapped in a thin silk cloth, was the silver sword she had once hoped would never again see the light of day.

Drawing a deep breath, Angelia reached down and grasped the dark hilt of the blade. On one side stood a set of three blue sapphires, representing the colors of the house of Serenitas. On the other, etched in silver, was the mark of Koloso. She raised the blade, balancing its familiar weight as she rose from the floor and left the room to reemerge into the decaying training area, securing the secret door behind her. She walked to her left and stepped onto an old, faded mat. "So," she spoke to the silent room. "It has come to this at last."

She stood on the golden floor for a long time, staring down at the blade in her hand. Then turned it, pressing the edge against her palm. Blood swelled to the surface, transforming her skin from white to scarlet as it dripped from her hand to the faded mat. "May the Gods forgive me," she whispered.

Specks of light began to appear around her like glints of sunlight sparkling across a jewel. At first, they sparkled throughout the room, but then began to gather close together, like tiny fairies moving to cluster around her body. The lights grew in brilliance until they become blinding and Angelia was forced to close her eyes against them. Then, suddenly, they vanished. Angelia opened her eyes and traced her fingers over the smooth surface of her perfectly flawless skin.

The Story Continues In...

RISE OF THE TEMPLE GODS: HEIR TO THE DEFENDANTS

KYLE SAT IN HIS PRIVATE study attempting to read the papers stacked before him. As captain of the guard to the Crown Princess, it was his job to review any reported or perceived threat to her safety. However, his mind was far from the specific task at hand. The fear in Mary's eyes from the previous night had haunted him. *I know she is having trouble adjusting,* he thought. *But the fear. The absolute fear?*

She called the Gods. Ameria's words echoed through his mind. *And the Gods answered.*

Kyle knew something dark had transpired that night, but the action that resulted in his life at the cost of Marcus' was one that Mary was either unwilling or utterly incapable of speaking of. Her suffering pulled at his heart, driving him to entertain notions that would result in destroying all of his father's highly held notions of honor. His dreams also continued to plague him; he was dreaming more and more frequently about the two young men who seemed to be engaged in eternal combat, one always resulting in the death of the other. "What does it mean?"

He stood from the chair and walked closer to the large fire. Autumn was approaching and the nights were becoming cooler. He pushed his hands towards the rising flames, allowing their warmth to chase the chill from his cold skin. "Mary, what do I do?" he asked, although he already knew the answer. "Do I take you away from here? Do I sweep you into my arms and ensure that your sister will inherit the throne? My father is right. It would be so easy." He drew a deep breath. "Do I leave, surrendering you to the fate that the Gods have seen fit to bestow?"

Yet he knew that he could no more leave her than he could take her away. *She is a princess,* his father had stated. *The one fate from which she can never escape.*

He shook his head. "Mary," he whispered. "Mariana."

He watched the flames dance across the crumbling wood, the tips occasionally transforming from yellow to red, orange, and white. "Gods of Kale, hear my prayer. Guide me upon this path. Guide me to protect this woman who has embedded herself so deeply into my soul."

Then Kyle heard a deep, gruff voice answer through the shadows. "Beware calling the Gods, Lord of Koloso. Beware."

Acknowledgements & Thanks

I WOULD LIKE TO OFFER a special thanks to a few people who both assisted and supported me throughout the creation of this novel.

I would like to thank Scott of the Vancouver Taekwondo Academy for his assistance in my research; both through an extensive interview and allowing me to observe several of his classes. Second, to the instructors and students at East West Martial Arts of West Vancouver for also allowing me to observe their courses and for making themselves available to answer questions.

I would also like to thank my long time writing mentors, Kate and Mike for instilling within me a passion for writing and reminding me of that passion when it was needed most.

Also, to my writing partner, Jonny, for all the hours spent discussing the finer points of writing in that little coffee shop. A thanks as well to members of the Watling Street Writers group of St. Albans, who helped shape the direction of the beginning of this novel, offering both support and critique along the way.

Also to my promotional team, and especially Kim and Karen who have walked me through the media and promotional process from the beginning of this story.

To my family for their never-ending love and support. This never would have been completed without them.

I want to thank my illustrator Raven, who is responsible for the beautiful map that is featured at the beginning of this novel. Thank you for helping to bring the world of Kale to life in such vivid detail.

To my fabulous content editor, Melissa, who worked tirelessly through draft after draft to assist me in making this story the best it could be. I love working with you and appreciate all that

To my copy editor and cover designer, Skyla, who takes the jumbled pictures in my head and consistently turns them into beautiful covers. Your work is nothing short of marvelous! Thank you for being my friend and mentor on this journey.

About the Author

K.L. BONE HAS A MASTERS degree in in Modern Literary Cultures. An American, currently living in Ireland working toward her PhD with a focus in vampire and children's literature. She wrote her first short story at the age of fifteen and grew up with an equally great love of both classical literature and speculative fiction. Bone has spent the last few years as a bit of a world traveler, living in California, London, and most recently, Dublin. When not immersed in words, of her own creation or studies, you'll find Kristin traveling to mythical sites and Game of Thrones filming locations.

Follow her at: www.klbone.com
On Twitter: @kl_bone
Or on Facebook: https://www.facebook.com/klboneauthor

Made in the USA
San Bernardino, CA
30 November 2016